The Flamingo Feather

The Flamingo Feather

KIRK MUNROE

Adapted by William Kottmeyer, Director

Saint Louis Reading Clinic

Illustrated by Lee Hines

jM9268k

WEBSTER PUBLISHING COMPANY

St. Louis   Atlanta   Dallas   Pasadena

THE EVERYREADER SERIES

Ben Hur

Cases of Sherlock Holmes

The Count of Monte Cristo

The Flamingo Feather

The Gold Bug and Other Stories

Ivanhoe

Juarez

Men of Iron

Simon Bolivar

A Tale of Two Cities

Other Titles in Preparation

Copyright, 1949, by Webster Publishing Company.
Copyright in Great Britain and in the British Dominions and Possessions. Printed in U. S. A.

CONTENTS

Chapter 1—René Meets His Uncle	1
Chapter 2—The Voyage	4
Chapter 3—The Colonists Land	7
Chapter 4—René Saves a Friend	8
Chapter 5—The Wrestling Match	12
Chapter 6—Chitta's Revenge	17
Chapter 7—The Prisoner	20
Chapter 8—The Prisoner Escapes	23
Chapter 9—René Runs Away	29
Chapter 10—On the Trail	33
Chapter 11—Chitta Finds a Friend	38
Chapter 12—The Spies	42
Chapter 13—Trailing the Spies	45
Chapter 14—A Race for Life	48
Chapter 15—Trouble at the Fort	53
Chapter 16—Attack on the Fort	58

Chapter 17—René Gets Food 62

Chapter 18—René to the Rescue 66

Chapter 19—The Secret Tunnel 69

Chapter 20—Food for the Fort 72

Chapter 21—The Colony Gives Up 77

Chapter 22—Help Comes 80

Chapter 23—The Spanish Come 84

Chapter 24—Don Pedro Attacks 91

Chapter 25—Captured 96

Chapter 26—The Seminole Village 101

Chapter 27—E-chee Brings News 109

Chapter 28—Has-se to the Rescue 113

Chapter 29—The Escape 116

Chapter 30—A Faithful Friend Dies . . . 121

Chapter 31—The French Come Again . . . 125

Chapter 32—René Joins the French 128

Chapter 33—Treasure! 133

Chapter 1. RENÉ MEETS HIS UNCLE

It was 1564. Young René de Veaux had just passed his sixteenth birthday. A month before, the terrible fever had swept France. René's father and mother had died. René was their only child. Only old Frank, his father's servant, was left.

The boy had one hope. In Paris lived his uncle, after whom he was named. So he wrote a letter to the Chevalier René de Laudonnière. The weeks passed as the lonely boy waited. The letters had to go by horseback. Just when he was sure no answer would come, a letter arrived. The uncle, too, was now alone. He wrote the boy to come quickly.

And so, on a cold winter day, René and Old Frank started for Paris. René turned, took a last look at his home. A lump came into his throat. The tears rolled down his cheeks. He wiped them away bravely.

"Frank," he said, "I can't help crying. I'm sorry. You will never see me cry again. From now on I'll be a man."

"Good boy!" said the old servant. "I know you will be a brave man. I'm glad we go to your uncle.

He will help make a man of you. We hear great stories about him. He has done great deeds."

"Tell me about him, Frank. He is my uncle, but I know little of him. What does he do? Is he famous? Is he really a great man?"

"Well, people say he is a brave sailor. About a year ago he came back from the New World. He sailed with Admiral Ribault. Ah, lad, that takes a brave man! To sail the great ocean to the New World! He tells strange tales of wonderful new lands and people. Folks say he will go soon again. He is to lead the ships and people himself this time. They will start a new colony."

The boy was eager to hear. He asked many questions. Old Frank answered as well as he could. But, like others, he knew little of the New World. He told the boy about the famous sailors. He told him strange stories of sea monsters which swallow whole ships. The boy's eyes shone. He drove his horse ahead faster.

It took a full week to get to Paris. Each day they rode long hours. Each short night they slept in the inns. René dreamed every night of ships and strange lands and adventure.

At last they arrived. Uncle René greeted the boy warmly. He liked the tall, strong lad's looks as soon as he saw him.

"Well, lad," he said, "I am glad you are here. You are big and strong. We'll soon make a man of you."

That evening the two talked far into the night. Old Frank had been right. Uncle René was getting ready for another voyage.

"To the New World?" asked the boy eagerly.

"To the New World," said the man.

"Uncle, may I go? Please let me go!" said the boy.

The older man smiled.

"You are just a boy," he said. "Most men don't dare. Will you not be afraid? The ocean is wide. The Indians are fierce. The Spaniards are our enemies. We may never get there. We may all be killed if we do."

René took his uncle's hand. "Please, Uncle!" he cried. "I'll work as hard as anybody. I won't be in the way. I'm not afraid."

"Well," smiled his uncle, "I would really be glad to have you. I hoped you would want to go. I wanted you to say so first. I'm getting old. I won't sail much longer. You may as well get started."

Chapter 2. THE VOYAGE

They spent the next three months getting ready. Young René took his share of the work. Each day he became more useful. Each day the old sailor gave the boy more work. He soon loved the boy as if he were his own son. The boy began to look on him as a father.

At last everything was ready. The food and guns were on board. The three ships stood ready. The colonists now came aboard. Laudonnière said good-bye to the King and Admiral Ribault. Ribault was to follow with more colonists a few months later.

On a bright May morning uncle and nephew stepped aboard. A good wind was blowing. The flags went up and the sails filled. The cannon boomed and the people waved good-bye. The three ships moved slowly out to the great ocean. René looked back to the shore. Then he turned and looked toward the ocean. His heart was beating wildly. At last his dreams had come true. He was sailing for the New World!

Week after week they sailed west. They saw no other ships. Each day brought only sea and sky, sea and sky. But at last, on June 22, the lookout cried, "Land, ho!" The men scrambled to the deck to look. They shouted and crowded forward. René looked eagerly. Far away he could see a dim blue line. Slowly it grew clearer.

The ships seemed to crawl. As the sun rose, René could see palm trees and tall pines. He listened carefully. Far away he heard the waves booming against the land.

By noon the ships were as close as they dared go. The men let down the anchors and pulled up sail. René wondered how they would ever land. A long sand bar lay before them. The great waves roared.

Laudonnière was looking keenly at the shore.

"Behind that bar is smooth water," he said. "It leads into a broad river. I was here two years ago with Ribault. There is an Indian village over there. René, you come with me. You soldiers take another small boat. Follow us."

René and his uncle pulled for shore. Just as he thought the waves would smash their boat, his uncle steered through the bar. They shot through to still water. Before them lay the Indian village. A crowd was on the beach, shaking their bows and arrows.

The Indians had seen the ships far off. White men's ships meant danger. The Indian fighters ran down to the beach. The women left their work in the fields. They got the children together and ran to the forest. But then they saw the French flag. They shouted for joy. The French had always been fair and kind. They loved the French as they hated the cruel Spaniards. They called the women and children back. The men washed their war paint off.

As the small boats came near, the Indians ran to meet them. Then they saw Laudonnière. They shouted a welcome. They helped pull the boats ashore. René's uncle took him by the hand. They made their way to the chief's hut. He stood waiting.

René looked around with wide open eyes. He had never seen palm trees before. Bright colored birds flew here and there. The village was made up of strange looking huts. The brown Indians trooped beside them.

The Indians looked with as much interest at him. They had seen the bearded white men before. René was the first white boy, though, to come to their shores. The Indians thought all white men had beards and short hair. René had long yellow hair which hung to his shoulders. The old chief took a fancy to the white boy.

"Ta-lah," he said, pointing to the uncle. Ta-lah meant a palm. The Indians had given him that name two years before. Now the chief pointed to René.

"Ta-lah-lo-ko," he said. That meant "little palm."

And the Indians called him that ever afterwards.

The chief wanted them to stay. René's uncle said they could not. Their own white chief said they should go to the River of May. There they must build a fort for their colony. The chief then brought out presents. The white men gave presents to the Indians. They got back into their boats and rowed back to the ships.

Chapter 3. THE COLONISTS LAND

The sails rose again. During the night they sailed forty miles north. By daylight they saw the mouth of the River of May. They crossed the bar and sailed up the river.

Indian runners had already brought news of their coming. The Indian chief here was called Micco. When the Frenchmen landed, Micco and his people met them. The Indians shouted to see their white friends again. Micco led them to the top of a hill. Here, two years before, Admiral Ribault had set a stone with the French coat of arms. Micco pointed to the stone. The Indians had piled flowers over it and set baskets of corn around it. René could see they were trying to show they were friendly.

René's uncle looked the ground over carefully. He picked a spot near the hill.

"Here we will build the fort," he said. "We will call it Fort Caroline to honor our King Charles IX. This will be our colony."

Now the men brought the food and guns ashore. The empty ships turned back for France. The little army of white men was alone in the great unknown land. René's uncle was their leader. René stayed with him, of course. And that is how René became the hero of the adventures told in this book.

Chapter 4. RENÉ SAVES A FRIEND

The building of Fort Caroline took three months. The friendly Indians helped. First the men cut the biggest trees they could find. They set them deep into the ground close together. The thick trunks made a strong, high wall. Next they dug a deep ditch around the fort. They piled the dirt inside against the walls. Now they rolled their cannon up and pointed them over the wall.

While the work went on, René got to know Micco's son. He was a young Indian about René's age, named Has-se. They were soon good friends.

Before long René learned to speak Indian and Has-se learned René's French.

René's uncle, busy as he was, took time to teach the boy. Every morning René took his lessons with the sword and cross bow. In the evening Jack Le Moyne, the artist, taught him to draw.

René had the afternoons to himself. He went into the woods with his friend Has-se. The Indian boy showed him all his people knew. René was eager to learn. Before long he could follow a trail as well as his friend. He learned to hunt and to fish.

Has-se was a happy, friendly lad. Almost all the Indians liked him. But he had one bitter enemy. This enemy was a young Indian named Chitta. Chitta, in Indian, meant "snake." Has-se and Chitta had long been enemies. Neither could remember how the trouble had started. Has-se had never done him any harm. But Chitta saw that the other Indians liked Has-se. He knew, too, that they did not like him very much.

One afternoon Has-se asked René to go with him.

"I have something to tell you," he said. "I want no others to hear."

The boys pushed Has-se's canoe into the river and stepped in. René laid his cross bow beside him and climbed to the front. The boys paddled down the river to a small side stream. Here they turned in.

Great trees hung far over the water. They let the canoe float while Has-se talked.

"My friend," said Has-se, "we Indians will soon have a great day. This is the day of the Ripe Corn Dance. It is the big feast day of my people. There will be contests for the boys. The winner will be the bow bearer to Micco, my father, the chief. This is a great honor. When a boy is bow bearer a year, he becomes a warrior."

"What are the contests, Has-se?" asked René.

"First, shooting with bow and arrow. Next, throwing the spear. Then running and wrestling."

"And you want to win?"

"More than anything else. I have trained long and hard. But Chitta will try, too. He is older and stronger than I. I can run and shoot and throw the spear. In that I do not fear him. But he is big and heavy. I think he will beat me in wrestling. Ta-lah-lo-ko, you are my friend. Your people are wise. They are good fighters. Can you help me?"

"I can, Has-se," cried René. "Oh, I am glad you asked me. Listen. Just a week ago I helped Simon, our armor maker. He showed me a wrestling trick I never saw before. I have tried it every day. And it works! I will show it to you."

As they talked, the canoe floated near the shore. It stopped under a great branch. Long vines hung down to the water. Suddenly René reached out and jerked the canoe forward. At the same moment a great brown body dived like a shot from the tree. It hit the water just behind Has-se.

The animal was a great panther. René had seen his tail move just before he jumped for Has-se's bare back. René's quick move saved Has-se and sent the panther into the river. But it missed by only a few feet. It rose to the top close beside them.

Has-se grabbed his paddle. He pushed the canoe ahead—but right into the vines. The boys could not get it free. The panther began to swim toward them.

René slipped an arrow into his cross bow. He shot, hit the panther on the shoulder. The blood spurted, making the water red. The animal snarled and clawed the canoe. René grabbed another arrow and shot again. This time he missed. The panther was almost upon them. The boys turned to jump.

Suddenly a great dark form rose from the water behind the panther. A pair of terrible jaws opened wide—and snapped shut. The panther screamed. His claws scraped the canoe. Then the water closed over his head. Down, down he went. A few bubbles came up. Then all was still. The boys sat as if they were frozen. At last René spoke.

"What was it?" he asked weakly.

"Alligator," said Has-se.

Chapter 5. THE WRESTLING MATCH

René's uncle was worried when he heard the story.

"My boy," he said, "you must be more careful. Don't go into the woods alone again. The woods are no place for a white boy. You are not an Indian yet." He did not tell him to stop going with Has-se, though. He wanted to stay friendly with the Indians. The white men got most of their food from their Indian friends. Laudonnière was glad that René and Has-se were friends.

The next afternoon Has-se came looking for René.

"My friend," he said, "you said you would show me a wrestling trick. I have come for my lesson."

"I will show it to you, Has-se," said René. "But you must never show it to anyone else."

René took him into an empty room. The trick was simple. You leaned back as though you were going down. Then you slipped a leg forward quickly and tripped your man. It was easy, but it worked every time. Anyone who did not know it would fall. Has-se learned it quickly.

"Thank you, René," he said. His eyes showed how thankful he was.

A few days later the Indians got ready for their great Dance of the Ripe Corn. They laid out the race course first. They cleared the bushes away and mixed clay into the sand. Then they stamped the ground smooth and flat. A big tent was raised for the chiefs and white men. They tried their bows and put new strings on them. Those who were lucky enough to have steel and iron made new arrow heads. Has-se showed René his new spear. Indians came in from far and near. Soon hundreds were camping near Fort Caroline.

The feast day came at last. Soon after breakfast the white men marched over to see the games. Micco and his people welcomed them warmly. They asked their white friends to sit in the big tent to watch. Micco waved his hand to begin the games.

First came the races for wives. The young Indian men could marry only on this day. The Indian girls were given a big start. If they wanted to, they could easily get away to the goal. Usually they let themselves get caught. The girl would marry the young man who caught her. This day a young Indian chief called Eagle caught Day Star, Has-se's beautiful sister.

Next came the boys' games. About twenty lads stepped forward. The tallest was Chitta, the Snake. The best looking boy was Has-se. In his dark hair he wore a red flamingo feather. Only a chief's son could wear the flamingo feather.

Everybody soon saw either Chitta or Has-se would win. Both were far better than the others, but these two were evenly matched. Has-se won the first contest—throwing the spear. Chitta got a good start in the foot race and held his lead all the way. The race was close, but Chitta won by a step. Both shot so well with the bow, the judges had to call it a tie. And so they came to the last contest—the wrestling match.

They faced each other carefully. Chitta was taller and heavier than Has-se. The match did not seem fair. Suddenly Chitta leaped forward and threw his weight on Has-se. The smaller boy fell heavily to the ground. And so Chitta won the first fall.

The two faced each other again. This time Has-se stepped lightly around Chitta. Chitta moved in slowly and reached out for a hold. Has-se slipped his arms around Chitta and held tight. Now Chitta threw himself forward, trying to force Has-se down. Has-se held a moment and then seemed to weaken. He bent backward—and suddenly Chitta crashed to the ground. No one seemed to know what had happened. Chitta slowly got up and shook his head. Only René had seen Has-se's leg flash out and trip his enemy just before Chitta fell.

15

Again they got their holds. They pulled and pushed until the sweat rolled down their bodies. Chitta slowly forced Has-se back again. It seemed as though René's friend must give up. He started back as he had before—and again Chitta landed flat. Has-se stepped back, a proud smile on his face. He was winner of the games and would be his father's bow bearer.

But Has-se had to pass one more test—the black drink. The Indian medicine men made a secret drink of roots and leaves. He who drank it would feel terrible pains. One who drank it was to show how brave he was. He must keep smiling and not show his pain. If he cried out, he had to do women's work. He could never fight or hunt or be with the Indian warriors.

So now Has-se sat himself on a high seat. The Indians crowded near to watch. A medicine man came forward and handed him the bowl. Has-se took the bowl, looked at his people, and swallowed the drink. Then he folded his arms and smiled. For fifteen minutes he sat there, not moving. The smile never left his face. Great drops of sweat poured over his face. A shout from the Indians told him when the time was up. Then, weak and sick, he arose. The medicine men led him away through the crowd of friendly Indians. Has-se had passed his test.

René ran after him to shake his hand. Indians and whites shouted and cheered. Everybody was glad that the boy had won. Everybody, that is, but Chitta. He turned away, shamed and angry.

"I'll get him," he snarled. "And I'll get those that shout for him. Indian or pale face—I'll pay them back."

Chapter 6. CHITTA'S REVENGE

So Has-se became bow bearer to Micco, his father. Somehow Chitta guessed that René had shown Has-se the wrestling trick. He hated René almost as much as he hated Has-se. But Chitta was like his name—a snake. He could wait to strike a deadly blow. After the games Chitta was seen no more.

As soon as the games ended, the feast started. The Indians sang and danced far into the night.

At last the dancers began to tire. The drum beaters got sleepy. The music sounded weaker and softer. Finally it stopped. Two hours past midnight the whole camp was asleep. Even the guards dozed. The only sound was the hooting of an owl.

Had the guards been awake, they might have seen a man's moving shadow. It came from the dark forest. It moved slowly to the great store house which held the Indians' winter food. The store house was built of wood and palm leaves. The summer sun had dried it out.

The shadow moved closer. It crawled like a snake past the open places lit up by the moon. It carried a covered shell. Inside the shell, on sand, lay live fire coals. In the other hand the shadow held pine sticks which would burn like gunpowder.

At last the shadow reached the store house. Still the sleepy guards saw nothing, heard nothing. Now the wall hid him. He stooped and covered his shell with a robe. He held the pine sticks to the coals, blew on them. They smoked a moment, then burst into flames.

The man now held the burning sticks to the palm roof. It sprang into flame. He ran down the side, lighting the roof in a dozen places. He turned and threw the sticks on the roof. Now he ran for the dark forest, giving a loud, shrill scream.

By the time the guards saw the flames, the whole store house was burning. The other Indians now awoke and ran toward the fire. They could only stand there, helpless, and watch. The flames leaped and roared. In a few minutes the store house and food were ashes. All asked how it had happened. No one knew. Even the guards could not guess.

Has-se had slept through the feast. Weak and sick from the black drink, he had lain as if he were dead. When he awoke, the feast was over. Sleepy no longer, he had slipped into the forest. A clear stream ran not far from the edge. There he went to get a drink. He lay on the bank a while, feeling better but still weak. Suddenly he heard a shrill scream. When the flames rose he got to his feet and hurried back. He knew something must be wrong.

He moved quietly through the woods. As he came to the edge of the forest he stopped. He saw in a moment what had happened. Just as he was going to yell a warning, a shadow moved against the flames. The shadow of an Indian stood straight before him. His arms were folded and he faced the burning camp. Has-se could have reached out and touched him. Suddenly Has-se heard him laugh softly. The Indian raised his fist and shook it. Then he spoke.

"The white man and the red man shall learn to fear Chitta, the Snake."

Has-se could hardly believe his ears.

"What! Is this your work, Chitta? Do you do this to your own people?" he cried.

Chitta knew Has-se's voice. Like a flash he turned and smashed him full in the face. Has-se, still weak, went down. As he fell his head hit a tree root.

"Lie there, bow bearer," snarled Chitta. "I have no time to kill you now. I'll get you later." He sprang into the forest and was gone.

When Has-se came to, he was in his father's tent. It was now broad daylight. Day Star, Has-se's sister, was bathing his head with cold water. As Has-se opened his eyes, his sister bent over him.

"Brother," she said, "who hit you? What happened?"

"Chitta the Snake," he answered weakly.

"And the store house?"

"Chitta," he said again.

She sprang to her feet and called Micco.

"Chitta has done this thing, my father."

The chief called out the news to his people. A great angry cry arose. It would be a bad day for Chitta if Micco's people ever caught him.

Chapter 7. THE PRISONER

Losing their winter's food was a great blow to the Indians. It was even worse for the white men. René's uncle had just bought the greater part from Micco. There was not much food in the fort. There were animals in the forest and fish in the rivers, of course.

But the Frenchmen were not good at hunting or fishing. They were used to getting their food from their Indian friends.

Two days later the white men got another surprise. They noticed there had been no Indians near the fort. Scouts went to the Indian camp to see what was wrong. They soon came hurrying back. Not an Indian was there. Every one of Micco's people was gone.

René's uncle was worried. His men were worn out from building the fort. Many had caught the fever. The fever brought pains in the arms and legs and laid the men up. Now the winter's food was gone. The Indians who might have helped by hunting and fishing were gone. His men were new to the country. They could work, but outside the fort they were helpless.

The men did not seem to be worried. They thought Ribault would come with help. Laudonnière knew he would not be there for several months. He himself was worn out with work and worry. He had been feeling the fever come on him lately, too. That worried him most of all. If he were laid up, things could be very bad.

There was only one thing to do. They must have a meeting and talk it over. Laudonnière called his men in. He told them of the danger.

"Men," he said, "we are in a bad spot. You may as well know it. I had just closed a deal with Micco to get our winter's food. The fire cleaned them out and cleaned us out."

"But the ships—" said one. "Ribault will soon be here."

"We cannot look for Ribault for months. We do not even know if he will be on time. A few storms —and he may not even come."

René looked closely at his uncle. He knew he must be worried to call them in.

"The Indians are gone," said Laudonnière. "Where, I do not know. They have gone without a word. I have told the guards to watch for Indians. If they see one, they will bring him in."

Just then someone knocked on the door. René jumped up and opened it. Two soldiers stood there. Between them was a young Indian. A soldier had hold of each arm.

"Has-se!" cried René. "Uncle, it is Has-se, Micco's son, my friend."

"Bring him in," said Laudonnière.

Chapter 8. THE PRISONER ESCAPES

The guard stepped in and saluted.

"Sir," he said, "we saw this fellow in the woods. He was hanging around watching the fort. We sent some men out the back gate. They got behind him and spread out. They caught him just as he was slipping away. Fought like a wildcat, he did. We tied him up and here he is."

"Good. You may go. Stay outside the door, though. René, you sit down."

The soldiers left. The young Indian stood straight before them. He folded his arms and did not move. René tried to catch his eye, but Has-se would not look. He was dressed as a warrior. The flamingo feather shone bright in his hair. His face was proud and fearless. He said nothing, but looked at Laudonnière.

The old man smiled at the handsome lad. "Now, son," he said, "where are your people? Why did they go? Why are you spying on us?"

The young Indian's eyes flashed. He spoke in French.

"My name is Has-se. I am a chief's son. My father

and our people have been friendly. This is our country. We go where we please. We go when we wish. We stay when we wish. You have no right to bring me here. I will answer no questions until you set me free. Has-se has spoken."

René was proud as he heard Has-se's brave speech. Laudonnière liked the boy's bravery, too. But he kept asking questions. Where had they gone? Where were the Indians now? Why had they gone? Has-se would give him no answer.

"Has-se has spoken," he said. Not another word could they get out of him.

At last René's uncle called the guards back.

"Take him to the guard house," he said. "Lock him in carefully. Do not let him escape."

When Has-se had gone, he turned to the others.

"Well," he said, "what shall we do with him?"

"Set him free," said Le Moyne. "The Indians are our friends. They always have been. Why should we make enemies of them? This lad will talk only if we free him. I say, free him."

René jumped up.

"That's right," he cried. "Has-se is my dear friend. We have no right to hold him. I say—"

"Now, just a minute, René," said his uncle. "I don't mind that you stand up for your friend. Maybe he has done no wrong. But you are among older men who are wiser than you. Remember you are just a boy. When we want a speech, we can ask for it."

René sat down, his face red. Then his uncle said, "I think we should free him, too. We must be kind to him. We cannot make enemies of his people. What do you others think?"

"I think we should keep him," said one. "Let's hold him in the guard house. We can tell the Indians we have him. If they bring us food, the boy goes free. If they don't, we keep him."

"I think he's right," said another. "I say hold him."

"I think you're wrong," said Laudonnière. "But since we don't agree, let's hold him another day. We can talk it over again. René can go see him. Maybe he will tell René why the Indians left."

René found his friend in the guard house. Has-se sat in a corner, holding his face in his hands.

René closed the door carefully and came over to him. He threw his arm around Has-se's neck.

"Surely, Has-se," he said, "you do not think me your enemy?"

Has-se put his hand on René's shoulder.

"I know you are my friend, Ta-lah-lo-ko. I should know you would not be against me. But your people put me here. They have no right to put me here."

The boys sat down on a bench.

"Tell me, Has-se," said René, "why did your people leave?"

"That is no secret," said Has-se. "I would not tell because they tried to make me tell. I will tell you. We have no food. Our friends, the Alachua Indians, have much food. We go to our friends until the next corn planting. Micco, my father, feared the white men would keep our hunters here. He knows the white men can not hunt. My father wants no trouble with your people. We are brothers."

"He is your chief," said René. "He must do what is best. But why did you not go with them? Why are you here at the fort?"

"To see you, Ta-lah-lo-ko. I wanted to tell you why we go. I wanted to warn you of Chitta. Chitta is now your enemy, too. He has sworn to kill you."

"To kill me? Why?" asked René. "What have I done?"

"I know not," said Has-se. "I think he knows you showed me the wrestling trick. He wanted to be bow bearer."

"That may be," said René. "I don't know how he could have found out. But why does he wish to kill me for that?"

"Ah, Ta-lah-lo-ko, you do not know Chitta. He is like a snake. He will risk his life to get you. It was Chitta who burned down the store house."

"I am glad you told me. I will be ready for him. I do not fear him."

"Now there is something else," said Has-se. "I know your people have no food. You will soon be hungry. There is no food in this country. The Alachuas have plenty. If one of you would go with me, you might get some. You could bring things to trade. If many white men came, the Indians would be afraid. If one comes, they would talk and trade. He could go with me. I would tell them he is a friend. Could you go with me, Ta-lah-lo-ko?"

"Why, I don't know what to say. You are not yet free, Has-se. How can you be sure you can go?"

Has-se smiled. "These walls cannot hold me. I go when I am ready. Will you go with me? Meet me two nights from now. Meet me where the panther jumped at us. I will see that no harm comes to you. You will get back to your people."

René wanted to talk more about the plan. Just then the guard came back.

"The sun goes down, Master René," he said. "Another guard will take my place soon. I must ask you to go. It does no good to talk to this stubborn young Indian."

René did not want the guard to see they were friendly. He said goodbye to Has-se. Then he added, "Maybe I'll see you tomorrow, maybe not."

The guard closed the door. "I should think not," he said. "Why talk to him at all? I would make slaves of all the Indians myself. I'd get a whip and—"

"Shut up!" cried René. "A whip, you say? Another word and you will get worse than a whip."

The next morning Has-se was gone. The guards looked through the fort, but found nothing. The guard came to tell René's uncle.

"I looked in at midnight," he said. "He was sleeping quietly. I looked again at sunrise. The room was empty. The guards at the gates have seen no one leave. They heard nothing during the night. I can see that he might get through the window. I can't see how he could get out of the fort. The gates are the only way out. This is Indian magic."

Laudonnière was not sorry the boy had escaped. He spoke to René.

"I'm glad your friend got away. I don't like the way it happened. I hope he comes to no harm. But I wish we could have sent some men with him. These Alachua Indians have food. We might have been able to get some. I wish we knew where they are. We could have used Has-se as a guide."

"Could I have gone, Uncle?" asked René.

"You? No, boy. You are too young. That would be a dangerous trip. We would have sent an older man."

Chapter 9. RENÉ RUNS AWAY

In one way René was glad to hear his uncle say what he did. He was glad to know Has-se's idea was a good one. He was sorry he would have to go without telling his uncle. He knew he was the one who had the best chance.

René thought about it all morning. There was only one answer. He must go. He must go and not tell anyone. There was no use asking his uncle to let him go. He would never agree.

So he got together some knives, mirrors, beads, and other things. He packed them together into a bundle. During the afternoon he slipped out and hid the bundle in the forest.

René did not know how Has-se had escaped. He knew, though, that his friend would keep his word. He would be at the meeting place. The moon would not rise until ten o'clock. He had plenty of time. His uncle was feeling the fever again and went to bed early. René told him good night.

About nine o'clock the boy left the house. He carried his cross bow over his shoulder. He walked down to the front gate. The guard stopped him.

"Who goes there? Oh, Master René, it is you."

"Just going out for a walk," said René.

"I'm sorry," said the guard. "You must not leave the fort. Nobody leaves the fort after sunset. Those are our orders since the Indian escaped."

René did not know what to do. If he climbed the wall, he might be shot. They would catch him crossing the big ditch if he did get over. He walked over to the shadows and sat down. There must be some way to get out.

As he sat thinking, the great bell struck ten o'clock. Now the guards would change. He heard their footsteps coming and going. René sat so close to the gate he could hear their voices. He thought he heard a voice he knew. He listened carefully. His friend Simon, the armor maker, was guarding the big gate. Here was his chance!

In a few minutes the guards walked past him. No one saw him sitting in the shadows. Their footsteps died away. All was quiet again.

Suddenly René heard someone groan. A moment later he heard it again. He got up and walked quietly to the gate. He laid his cross bow down against the wall. Then he went on.

"Who goes there?" called Simon.

"It is I, René, good Simon. I heard you groan. What is the matter? Are you sick? Can I help?"

"Ah, Master René," said Simon. "I guess the fever has got me. Everybody is getting it. I felt bad this afternoon. Le Moyne gave me some medicine. If you take it right away, it stops the pain. I left it in my room. This night air is cold. I feel the pains coming on again. Master René, will you get my medicine for me? It is on the table in my room."

But René had been thinking as Simon spoke. "Listen, Simon," he said, "you go. You know where it is. I don't. When you are there get yourself a heavy coat. You will be cold here tonight. I'll take your watch until you get back."

Simon did not want to go. No good soldier will leave his watch. But the night was cold and he was in pain.

"Well," he said at last, "I guess I'll have to do that. The pain is getting worse. Keep your eyes and ears open. I have never failed in my duty yet."

The old soldier handed René his spear. He limped slowly away to his room. As soon as Simon had gone, René picked up his cross bow. Then he quietly opened the big gate. He left it open a few inches. Now he took Simon's spear and walked before the gate. A few minutes later he heard footsteps.

"Is that you, Simon?" he called softly.

"Yes, lad," came the answer.

René laid down the spear and picked up his bow.

He slipped quietly out the gate and pushed it shut. He ran across the bridge. In a moment he was lost in the dark forest shadows.

The moon was full and bright, but René got over the bridge unseen. The old man looked around for the boy a few minutes. He called softly. No one answered.

"That boy!" he grumbled. "Trying to play tricks again."

He picked up his spear and began to march again.

René stopped. He reached into his coat and pulled out a note. He had written it before he left his room. Now he found a sharp stick. He stuck it through the note and jabbed it into the ground. It was to his uncle. This is what it said:

Dear Uncle:

I guess I am doing wrong. I am leaving because I want to help. But I was afraid you would say no. I am going to the Alachua camp. Has-se, my friend, goes with me. I shall try to get food from them. I saw you were worried. If I get through, I will be back in a month or so. If I never come back, please forgive me. You have always been good and kind. Nobody helped me get away. Nobody knows I am gone.

René

René pulled his belt tight, picked up his bow, and

turned into the forest. It was getting late. He stopped to pick up his hidden bundle and hurried on. Soon he came to the little stream. He gave the cry of an owl, as Has-se had taught him. The answer came back in a moment. Then he was standing next to his friend. Has-se led him to the canoe. In a few minutes they were shooting down the river.

Chapter 10. ON THE TRAIL

The boys' paddles flashed bright in the moonlight. The boat moved fast and quietly. René told Has-se how he had got away.

"I was afraid you would be gone," he said. "I came as fast as I could."

"You did well, Ta-lah-lo-ko," said Has-se. "I think the Great Spirit must be helping us."

René was not so sure. Had he done right? Should he have run away? He knew his uncle would worry.

"Has-se," he said, "now tell me how you got away. You were locked in. How did you do it? If you can get out easily, others could get in."

Has-se said nothing for a few minutes. At last he spoke.

"You are my brother. I want to hide nothing from

you. But I must not tell you now. Sometime I will tell you, though."

René was a little hurt. It seemed that Has-se did not trust him. But he knew his friend must have a good reason. So he asked no more about it and talked of other things.

At last they turned their boat toward the shore. They ran the boat on the bank and hid it in the tall grass. Has-se said they had better stay until the sun came up. He led the way to a small hut. The floor was piled with soft grass. The tired boys threw themselves down. In a few minutes they were fast asleep.

It seemed to René that he had just fallen asleep. But there stood Has-se shaking him. He jumped up. The sun was already high. He ran down to the beach and washed his face. Has-se had been up for an hour.

Breakfast over, they got into their canoe again. At noon they came to a big lake. They crossed and found the mouth of a wild, dark river. The next two days they spent going up the river. As they went on, it got narrower and darker. They paddled so hard and long that Has-se said they might soon catch his people.

Three or four times Has-se spotted places where canoes had landed. Here they stopped. They found camp fire ashes each time. Has-se looked worried. René asked what the matter was.

"What's troubling you, Has-se?" he asked. "You look worried. Can't you tell me?"

Has-se paddled a few minutes. Then he said:

"There are others following my people. I fear they are enemies."

"What makes you think so?"

"They stop where my people stop. They look at my people's camp fire ashes. Always they look after my people are gone. I have found their camp fire ashes on the other side of the river. There are two men. One man is very big. He wears strange moccasins. I fear they are enemies."

"But who would follow so big a band? And why? Two cannot hurt so many."

"I don't know. I fear they are the outlaw Seminoles. If they are, they are trying to rob them. Maybe they hope to catch one of my people alone. If they do, they will scalp him. They would not want an open fight. Or maybe one is an enemy of my people who has a friend to help him."

They were quiet a while. Then René said:

"Who are these Seminoles? I know you don't like them. Why?"

"Seminole means runaway. The Seminoles are thieves and killers—bad Indians. When we had bad

36

men we ran them out. Other Indians did the same. These bad Indians got together. They have grown until now they are a tribe. They fight all men. My people are at war with them. We will never smoke their peace pipe."

"And who is this enemy you talk about?"

"You should know, Ta-lah-lo-ko. I mean Chitta the Snake. I hope we do not meet him."

"If we do, we can handle him," cried René. "He had better let us alone."

"No, Ta-lah-lo-ko. I have a bad feeling. I fear trouble. I am not afraid of him, either, but I have a bad feeling."

While they talked, the river had got still narrower. Now they were in a dark swamp. The little stream ran into muddy pools. As they came to one of these, they looked ahead. Both boys saw something move ahead of them. In a moment it was gone.

"What was it?" asked René softly.

Has-se's mouth was closed tight.

"A canoe," he said. "We are close behind them."

Chapter 11. CHITTA FINDS A FRIEND

Who was in the canoe? Let us go back to the night after the Ripe Corn feast. That night Has-se had seen Chitta in the forest. Chitta had hit Has-se and knocked him out. Then he had run into the forest. He made his way to the river. Many canoes lay on the bank. Chitta looked them over quickly. He wanted a light, fast one. He saw what he wanted. Picking up a paddle, he jumped in. Down the river he went. In a few minutes he was gone.

He really hated the white men more than he hated his own people. He knew he was burning up the Indians' winter food. But he also knew the white men needed that food. Has-se's friend René he hated especially. Chitta had hoped to set the store house afire and get away. The Indians might never find out who had started the fire. At least, he thought, no one could prove anything. But then he had run into Has-se. Has-se knew he had done it. Now he would be an outlaw forever. He could never come back.

So now he hated Has-se more than ever. Always the Indians had liked Has-se and had not liked him. Then Has-se had beaten him in the games. Now he would tell who had burned the store house. Chitta ground his teeth to think of him. Some day he would get him. Some day he would kill him.

Chitta paddled until he came to the big hill where Ribault had set the stone. He hid the canoe in the bushes. A narrow path ran up to the top. Chitta found it and went up. By daylight he could see for miles around. If any one came after him, he would see them before they got close.

He fell asleep as soon as he lay down. About an hour later a tall Indian stepped from behind the bushes. Chitta had seen or heard no one. The Indian had watched him come and lie down. For an hour he had waited to see if others would come. Now he quietly crept toward the sleeping Chitta. In his hands he held a deer hide rope.

Quiet as a cat, he knelt beside Chitta. He slipped the rope around Chitta's feet. Chitta kept snoring softly. The Indian tied the other end of the rope to a tree. Then he sat down quietly and waited for Chitta to wake up.

Just as the sun rose, Chitta rolled over. He opened his eyes, threw off his robe, and sat up. Then he saw the big Indian. He gave a sharp cry and jumped up. As he did, the rope tripped him. He fell flat. The Indian now jumped up and stood over him. A cruel smile lighted his dark face.

But Chitta was no coward. He saw the Indian had him. He looked up calmly.

"Who are you? What do you want?"

The tall Indian smiled.

"First I will tell you something about yourself. Your name is Chitta. Yesterday you were at the Ripe Corn feast. You were in the games. The boy with the flamingo feather beat you. You were angry. You wanted to get even. So you set fire to the store house. Now you are an outlaw—like me. I am Cat-sha the Tiger. I am a Seminole."

Chitta's eyes got wide. He had never seen Cat-sha, but he had heard of him. Cat-sha was the cruelest and boldest of the Seminoles. Micco's braves had often told stories about him.

Cat-sha had once belonged to another tribe. Even as a boy he was fierce and cruel. One day he was playing with other Indian boys. Cat-sha got angry and smashed another boy's face. The boy died. His people drove Cat-sha away. Since that day he had been an outlaw. He grew bigger and stronger. Other outlaw Indians joined him. And so he became their chief. These Indians were the Seminoles Has-se had told René about. They were soon known as the cruelest and wildest tribe in the land. Chitta knew all this. His heart grew cold.

Cat-sha kept talking.

"I have watched the pale faces many days. I hate them. Gladly would I drive them away. That is why I am here. I watched your people sing and dance. I, too, was going to burn the store house. I am glad you did it for me. Had you not done it, I would kill you now. Now I may spare your life. Come with me. Join my band. Do so and you live. Say no and you die."

"Become a Seminole!" cried Chitta. He hated the white men and he hated his own people. But never had he thought of joining the hated Seminoles.

Cat-sha's eyes blazed angrily.

"Yes," he cried. "Why not? Are you not an outlaw? Do you not run away from your own people? Where can you go? No one will have you but the brave and warlike Seminoles! If you don't join, I'll kill you now. We Seminoles know only two kinds of men. One is for us. The other is against us. Make up your mind. What kind are you?"

Chitta knew what he must do. He would join them. If he did not, he would die. Chitta was not ready to die. He looked up at the big Seminole chief. He spoke bitterly.

"So be it, Cat-sha. Call me Chitta the Seminole. I am Chitta the Snake. Well, I shall be a Seminole snake. I shall bite the Seminoles' enemies now."

Cat-sha smiled. He stooped down and loosened

the rope. He helped Chitta get up. Then he put his arm around him.

"Chitta the Seminole," he said, "I welcome you. I am glad to have you. Listen to me! Some day we shall be a great, strong tribe. All men shall fear us. You will be proud you are a Seminole. I, Cat-sha the Tiger, have spoken."

Chapter 12. THE SPIES

Cat-sha got out some dried deer meat. The two new friends sat down behind some bushes and ate. As they did, they watched the river far below for enemies. Cat-sha spoke:

"My band waits in the great swamp. I have watched the white men's fort. I know we can surprise the fort and take it. When I was going back to get my men, many Indians came for the Ripe Corn feast. I knew these Indians like the white men and would help them. I must wait until they all leave again. When the white men are alone, my Seminoles shall strike."

"Ha!" cried Chitta. "I am not yet a great warrior, but I can help!" Then he told Cat-sha a secret only a few Indians knew. He himself had found out by chance. It was the same secret Has-se used to escape from the fort.

Cat-sha listened eagerly. He smiled and patted Chitta's shoulder.

"Well done, my young brave!" he said. "You are a great help to us. What you tell me will surely beat them. We can easily take the fort now. Let the white men take care! Before many days Cat-sha the Tiger and Chitta the Snake will jump at their throats."

Now Chitta pointed down to the river. Something was coming down the stream close to the bank. Cat-sha looked carefully.

"Canoes," he said. "There are many canoes. They are Indians. It looks like Micco's people."

It was Micco's people. Micco himself was in the first canoe. They were going to their friends, the Alachuas. Chitta and Cat-sha could see them plainly now.

"Ha!" cried Chitta. "The women and children go, too."

"Yes," said Cat-sha. "They take everything along. Their tents and blankets go, too. They are leaving for a long time. The Alachuas are their friends. They are going that way."

Chitta watched them with hate in his eyes. He shook his fist at the canoes.

"This is your work, my friend," said Cat-sha. "You

have burned their food. Let us follow them. Then we can turn aside and get my Seminoles. We can come back and wipe out these pale faces."

Cat-sha and Chitta made their way down the hill. Chitta found his stolen canoe. By now Micco's Indians were almost out of sight. Cat-sha and Chitta started after them. They were careful not to show themselves, but they stayed close behind. When the other Indians camped on one bank, they camped on the other. As soon as they left, Cat-sha and Chitta looked at their camp fires. Always they watched to see that no one stayed behind to catch them.

Cat-sha was glad to see they were going toward the Seminole camp. The Seminoles lived deep in the great swamp.

"We come near my camp," he said to Chitta. "We could even fall upon Micco's people. They have their women and children. We could take everything they have."

"That's a good plan!" cried Chitta.

"We shall see," said Cat-sha. "Do not fear, Chitta. Your day will come."

Chapter 13. TRAILING THE SPIES

So it was Chitta's and Cat-sha's canoe which Has-se saw. It was their camp fires which Has-se had seen.

"Look," cried Has-se. "These may be my own people. If so, we have caught them. They may be the two who follow my people and spy on them. If they are the spies, I must find out. I must warn my people. But I must keep you out of danger."

"What?" cried René. "You must keep me out of danger? Why? We are friends. We are together. How can you keep me out of danger? If you are in danger, I am with you."

Has-se made no answer to this brave speech. He smiled at René. He knew René would stick with him.

There was open water before them. Has-se and René were still hidden by the trees ahead. No Indian would cross the open water in broad daylight. An enemy could lie in wait and cut him down.

But Has-se had just barely seen the canoe ahead. He was sure he and René had not been seen. The spies would be looking ahead.

Has-se took the chance. He and René crossed the open water as quickly as they could. As they came near, Has-se watched keenly. He saw nothing, heard nothing to worry him. Happy that they were not seen, the boys paddled on into the dark swamp.

But they were wrong. They had been seen. And that almost cost them their lives. The sly Cat-sha was like a tiger. Always he watched for danger. All men were his enemies. To stay alive he had to be watchful. He knew he must watch when he crossed open water. So this time, as he and Chitta crossed, he took a quick look backward. The light flashed on a moving paddle. He saw no more. But he knew some one followed them.

Cat-sha said nothing until they were safe in the dark shadows. Then he spoke:

"Keep paddling. Do not look back. Someone follows us."

"Follows us?" said Chitta. "Who can it be?"

"I do not know yet."

"Let us turn aside and hide. When they come by we can see," said Chitta.

But Cat-sha was clever.

"No," he said. "Not yet. If they saw us, that is what they think we will do. They will watch carefully. When they find we are not waiting there, they will think we did not see them. They will come on quickly."

"What shall we do then?" asked Chitta.

"We will go on about a mile. When we see a good spot we will stop and hide."

So they went on about a mile. They came to a good place where the vines hung over the stream. The canoe could barely get through.

"This is a good place," said Cat-sha. "Pull over. We hide here."

They lifted the canoe out and hid it among the vines. Cat-sha got behind the bushes on one side, Chitta on the other. They got their bows ready. Each fitted an arrow to his bow. They sat down to wait.

René and Has-se paddled slowly toward the trap. Not a leaf moved. There would be no warning. It seemed they would surely be caught. But Has-se knew how Indians like to surprise an enemy.

"Keep your eyes and ears wide open, Ta-lah-lo-ko," he whispered. "This is a bad place."

"I know it," said René. "Listen! What is that?"

A twig had snapped. The boys held their paddles up a moment and listened. The canoe drifted. It bumped gently against a sunken log. René reached his hand down into the water to push it clear. Suddenly he pulled it back with a cry of pain and fear. A large water snake, a moccasin, darted away.

Chapter 14. A RACE FOR LIFE

Has-se turned quickly when René cried out. He looked just in time to see the moccasin.

"Quick!" he cried. "Did it bite you?"

René held up his hand. Blood ran from his finger. He could not answer.

Has-se scrambled to his side. He pulled out a little, sharp dagger. Calmly he cut the bite larger. The blood now flowed freely. He put René's finger to his own mouth and began to suck out the poison. He spit it out and washed his mouth with water.

He got as much out as he could. Then he packed some river mud on the wound.

"Hold it there," he said.

He picked up the paddle and turned the canoe. Now he paddled to the open water. There grew a certain kind of water lily he knew well. He pulled some up by the roots. He picked out one of the roots and pounded it with the paddle. Taking René's hand he washed off the mud and put the lily root in its place.

The hand was swollen and it hurt badly. When Has-se put the root on, the pain began to go away.

"The pain is leaving already," René said.

"It is nothing," said Has-se. "This is what my people use for the snake bite." He smiled. "You see, the pale faces are wise in many things. They know things we poor red men know nothing about. But we have learned a little. We know there is a good thing for every bad one. Where there lives a deadly snake, there grows a healing plant. Do not fear. Soon your hand will be well.

"Now you must stay still. Keep the root there and wet your hand with cool water. I have something to do. A path goes through here which leads to this stream again. It is a short cut. You stay here and care for your hand. I will run down and see who these spies are as they pass."

"Go," said René. "I'll be all right. Be careful."

Their canoe was well hidden in the vines. René dipped his hand and kept it cool as Has-se had said. His thoughts went back to his uncle and the fort. He wondered how things were going there. Did they still have some food? Was his uncle angry?

Suddenly he heard a splash. A voice spoke. Raising his head slowly, René looked through the vines. Another canoe came up the stream. Two Indians were paddling. They stopped near his hiding place. One pointed to the vines. It was Chitta.

"Could they be in there?" he asked.

The other, a big dark Indian, shook his head.

"I don't think so," he said. "They must be back farther."

René's heart beat hard. He watched them, glad the thick vines hid him well. The Indians now went on up the stream. René let out a deep breath. He wished Has-se would hurry back.

René kept watching the stream. Chitta and the other Indian might come back. He did not hear Has-se's step until he was there. Has-se was suddenly beside him. René looked up and almost upset the canoe.

"Oh, Has-se," he whispered, "I'm glad you are back. Chitta is after us. He has a big strong Indian with him."

He told Has-se what had happened. Has-se listened until he was finished.

"I have some news, too," he said. "My people are down the river. They are not very far away. If we get there we will be safe. Let us go to them."

"But if we start, will Chitta and his friend not see us?"

"Maybe we can get started before they see us. They will have to be fast to catch us. How is your hand? Does the bite still hurt? Can you paddle?"

"Oh, my hand? Why, no. I had forgotten about it. The lily root has healed it."

Slowly the boys got the canoe back out. They got

it past the open water. They began to breathe easier and headed down the river again.

Just as they got well started a terrible scream rang out. It came from behind them.

"What is it?" asked René.

"The war cry of Cat-sha the Tiger, chief of the Seminoles!" cried Has-se. "It is he with Chitta. Come, we cannot fight those two. If you are strong, show it now. They have seen us. Go for your life!"

The two boys bent over and dug their paddles deep. Their light canoe rushed forward. Past the dark trees and vines they fled. Not far behind came the enemy. They, too, were coming fast. A smile showed on Cat-sha's face. He was sure they would win this race.

Cat-sha and Chitta had waited in their hiding place. Had the snake not bitten René, the boys would have fallen into their trap. When they did not come, the Seminoles had started back to find them. Again they would have found them had Has-se not hidden René and gone ahead. So the Seminoles paddled slowly back, watching the shore. Finding no one, they turned back once more to follow Micco's people.

As they came to the open water again, René and Has-se were leaving it. Cat-sha had one quick look. Then he gave his war cry. Both he and Chitta had seen the bright flamingo feather in Has-se's hair. Both saw René's yellow hair. In a moment they knew who had followed them. Here was a great chance for Cat-sha. He could get Micco's son and the white chief's son.

Faster and faster flew the canoes. Has-se and René knew it was a race for life or death. The two boys had the lighter and faster canoe, but Cat-sha's strong arms made up the difference. For a time the boys held their own. Then Cat-sha's power began to tell. Slowly the big canoe gained. Foot by foot it came closer and closer. Now the boys began to pant. Sweat rolled down their faces.

Suddenly Has-se stopped a moment. Putting his hand to his mouth, he gave a long shrill cry. It was the war cry of Micco's people. It rang loud and clear through the still swamp.

He took a quick backward look. The other canoe was almost upon them. Then, close by, there came an answer to Has-se's call. The war cry of Micco's people rang out again. Micco's warriors had heard and were coming!

Cat-sha knew then it was too late. Snarling, he picked up his bow and fitted an arrow to it. Kneeling in the canoe he took careful aim. The arrow whizzed so close to Has-se's head that it cut the red feather from his hair. It passed on and buried itself in René's shoulder. At that moment a great war canoe came into sight. Micco's warriors gave a shout as they saw the two canoes. The two tired and hunted boys dropped their paddles. They were safe!

Chapter 15. TROUBLE AT THE FORT

While all this was going on, things were happening at the fort. First, there was not enough food. Second, there was trouble among the French themselves. Third, there was danger of war.

Before René left, his uncle had sent out ten men. These men were to explore the country south of the fort. What they really wanted was gold. That is what many white men wanted in America. The kings of the Old World countries wanted to start colonies. They hoped to send hard workers who would build good colonies.

But many who wanted to come wanted only to get rich. They did not want to work. People told wonderful stories about America. Some thought that the mountains were made of gold. They thought they could chip off the gold and become rich. Of course, they wanted to bring it back home and never work again. Others said you could find jewels on the seashore. All you had to do was pick them up. When they found this was not true, they wanted to leave.

The ten men had now been gone from the fort a month. They had crossed deep rivers. They had lost themselves in the great dark swamps. All around them were birds of beautiful colors. There were strange and wonderful flowers. Many of the wild animals they had never seen before. But they did not care for these things. They wanted gold. Look as they might, they could find none.

So they were ten sad men. Their clothes were torn and ragged. Some were sick. All were hungry. At last they came to an Indian village. These Indians had never seen white men before. When they saw them, they ran. The hungry soldiers rushed into the Indian huts. They took all the food they could find. Then they built a great fire and cooked themselves a feast. So foolish and careless they were that they did not watch the fire. While they stuffed themselves, a hut caught fire. The flames jumped from one hut to another. In a few minutes the whole village was burning.

The Indians watched from the forest. When they saw their homes burning, they became very angry. They had not harmed the white men. They would have been glad to give them food. The white men had shown themselves to be enemies. The Indians began to shoot at them. One man fell dead. Several others were wounded. As the arrows kept falling around them, they ran. The Indians followed like shadows. Before they got back to Fort Caroline, four more paid their lives. A few days later five starved and ragged men stumbled into the fort. They had put all the southern Indians on the warpath against the whites.

This was more bad news for René's uncle. He had worried about the boy since he left. By now he was sure René was dead. He had no food for his men. Already fighting the fever, he found this last bad news too much. The fever overcame him. His men had to put him to bed.

Most of the men were sorry about his sickness. But others, especially those who hated work, now saw a chance to do what they wanted. These men, finding no gold, wanted a new leader. They wanted a leader who would take them back home. Laudonnière would never agree to that, as everyone knew. They hoped to build their own ship to sail to France.

The leader of these men was René's old friend Simon. He had always grumbled and growled. Then, when René had got away, Laudonnière had put him in the guard house. Simon did not like that. He had always been friendly with the grumblers. Now he went with them openly. When René's uncle got sick, he grew bolder.

Many of the other leaders were down with the fever, too. Laudonnière had to put Le Moyne in his place as leader. Le Moyne was no leader, but he did his best.

One morning he sat writing Laudonnière's orders. Someone knocked at his door. It was Simon, leading many of the colony. The old soldier saluted. Le Moyne saluted. He stayed on the door step. The others could not crowd into the room.

"Le Moyne," said Simon, "we want something. We want you to tell Laudonnière what we want."

"Well," he said, "what is it? Speak up and get back to work."

"Oh, I don't know," sneered Simon. "Maybe we won't get back to work at all. We are hungry."

"I know you have not much to eat. We hope for better things soon."

"We are dying of the fever."

"That is also partly true."

"The Indians will soon fight us."

"You have strong walls and guns."

"People back home have forgotten about us. We will rot here before help comes."

"Admiral Jean Ribault will never forget us. He said he would come. He will come."

"There is no gold here. Men cannot live in this land."

"Micco's people live here. They are strong and healthy. As for gold, we do not know. We have not found any yet. That does not prove there is none."

"Well," Simon said, "that's what we have to say. We are asking to have a ship built. We want to go back home. If Laudonnière is able, we ask him to lead us back."

"Men," said Le Moyne, "do not do this. This is foolish. You gave your word to stay. Your leader is sick. Go back to work. Wait a little longer."

"We want an answer now," said Simon. "We will not leave until we get it. Go ask him. Is that right, men?"

"That's right!" shouted the others.

"All right," said Le Moyne at last. He turned to take the message to Laudonnière.

The old man was lying in his bed. He turned weakly as Le Moyne came in.

"The men are outside, sir," said Le Moyne. "They are ready to give up. They want to build a ship. Simon speaks for them. He asks that you take us back."

Laudonnière tried his best to get up. He wanted to face the men who dared break their word. Finally he fell back on his pillow. He was too weak.

"Tell them NO!" he cried weakly. "I will not even think of it. Our king sent us here. I do what my king tells me. We stay until the king calls us back. Sick or well, I am leader here. Tell them to get back to work. The southern Indians may attack any minute. They must make the fort stronger. I will hear no more talk of our running away."

Le Moyne went back with the answer. Simon laughed.

"That is what we thought he would say. You can tell him we will fight the Indians. But tell him we are going to build a ship and we are going home. We don't care if he likes it or not. We have had only bad luck here. We are through."

Chapter 16. ATTACK ON THE FORT

Le Moyne went back to tell Laudonnière what had happened. The sick man got more excited than ever. His fever got worse. A little later he was out of his head.

Simon's men started right in building a ship. For the first time they worked hard. And they kept at it. In a month the body of the ship was finished. They were almost ready to get it into the water.

Now the men were at least doing something. Some were out looking for wood to make masts. Others were out looking for pitch to make the ship watertight. Still others were trying to hunt and fish to keep themselves alive. They needed to salt some fish and meat to get them home. Food was still their great need. The corn was now all gone. They were living on fish and palm buds.

Then the blow fell. It was just one month that René had been gone. The white men were outside the fort, doing their work. Suddenly a great band of Indians attacked them. The whites ran for the fort as fast as they could go. Many were killed and wounded. The Indians swarmed after them, up to the very gates. There the guards met them with heavy gun fire. The cannon saved the day. When they roared out, the Indians broke and ran.

Toward evening the Indians got ready to attack again. A great band gathered on a nearby hill. The white men could see them clearly from the fort. Simon had taken the lead in the fighting. Now he cried:

"Let's go out and get them! We can beat them. We do not have to hide behind walls."

He got the men ready to go. But the fever had laid many low. The Indians had already killed others. When Simon got them together, he had only

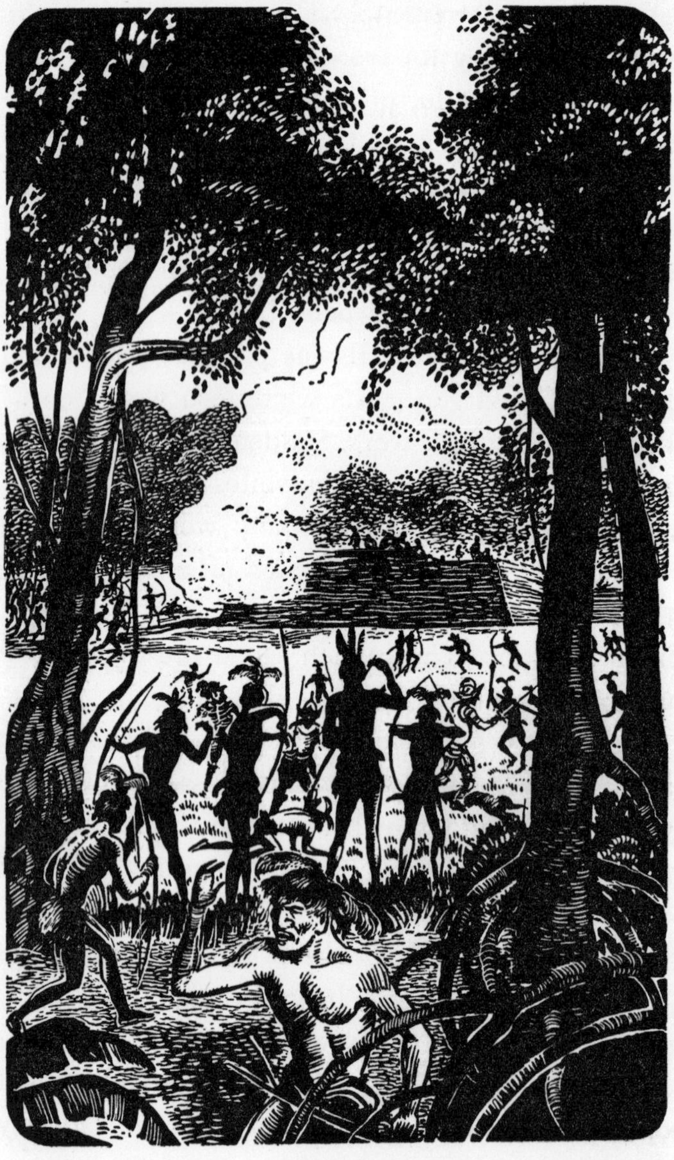

about fifty men. He thought he had enough. Like many others, he did not think Indians could fight.

Simon lined them up. He ordered the gate swung open. Out they marched, straight for the hill. The Indians stayed where they were. Simon got his men ready to charge.

But suddenly hundreds of Indians sprang from behind bushes and trees. The white men were surrounded. The band on the hill was only bait. Simon had fallen for an old Indian trick. The way to the fort was cut off. As they stood there, the arrows and spears began to mow them down. The terrible war cries rang through the air.

Simon's men were too surprised and scared to move for a minute. They could go only one way. They had one hope—to get back to the fort. It was fight or die—so they fought. They drew their swords and slowly hacked their way through. There did not seem to be a chance. One by one they dropped. Sweating and bleeding, the others fought on. Fresh Indians came howling to help.

At last it seemed the white men were through. Then, like magic, loud screams came from the Indians. Some one was attacking the Indians from the rear!

The soldiers did not stop to watch. The attack had given them a last chance.

"Charge!" screamed Simon. "Charge them! Back to the fort!"

Swords swinging, they made a last charge. The enemy broke. The soldiers crashed through. Scrambling, running, and even crawling, they got to the fort. The great gate swung open. They half ran, half fell in. The gate slammed shut.

And then from the forest they heard a clear voice crying, "France to the rescue! France to the rescue!" They looked at one another in wonder. Who could it be?

Chapter 17. RENÉ GETS FOOD

When the arrow hit René, he fainted. He and Has-se dropped their paddles and lay in their canoe. Everything went black before René's eyes. Then the Indians picked him up gently and carried him away. For a long time he knew nothing. At last he came to again. A soft hand was stroking his head. He looked up. It was Day Star, Has-se's sister.

He tried to get up. Day Star gently pushed him back and asked him to lie still a moment. She got up and left the tent. She came back quickly, bringing Has-se. Has-se told him what had happened.

Micco's warriors had stopped to find out who had been after them. Cat-sha and Chitta had paddled swiftly away. By the time Micco's men got going, the two were gone. They had got away in the great swamp. There even the Indians could not track them.

Day Star packed René's shoulder with healing roots. The Indian medicine worked wonders again. The next evening René was able to go outside. He lay before the chief's tent on a bear robe. A great fire was blazing. René and the Indians feasted on deer, turkey, and bear meat the hunters had brought in.

As René lay there, Has-se came to him. He took René's hand and opened it. Inside he put the flamingo feather the arrow had cut from his hair. René looked up in surprise. Has-se said:

"I give you the flamingo feather, Ta-lah-lo-ko. It means that we will always be friends. I want you to keep it. When you look at it, you will remember this day. Only a chief or a chief's son may give the flamingo feather away. If you ever need anything, send it back. When I or my people get it, we will do what you ask. This is our law. If you send the feather and ask us to die, we will do so. Keep it. Hide it. You may not wear it. Only my tribe's chief or his son may wear it."

"I thank you, Has-se. You are indeed my friend.

I will always keep it. I will never forget this day."

René looked at it closely. The feather was fastened to a fine, thin, gold chain. On the chain was a beautiful gold pin. Has-se had pinned the feather in his hair. Cat-sha's arrow had cut the chain.

Next morning they started moving again. Micco's people had enough food to get to the Alachuas. René and Has-se went with Day Star and Eagle, her husband. Has-se and Eagle paddled the canoe. René's arm was better, but still stiff and sore.

They reached the Alachuas' country two days later. Micco's people and the Alachuas spoke the same language. They had been warm friends for many years. The Alachua country was good. Great forests grew there. The water came from clear, cold springs. The streams were full of fish. The forests were rich in game. It was really a land of plenty. The Alachuas were kind and gentle people. When they saw Micco's people, they raised a welcoming shout.

To the Indians René was the white chief's son. As a chief's son, Micco asked him to stay in his tent. He slept on a bear skin with Has-se, his friend. It took another week to heal his wound. That was a happy week. Every day René learned more of the Indians' language. Day Star and Has-se taught him the words.

At the end of a week René's wound was healed.

"I am well again," he said to Has-se. "I must get back. My people must be very hungry. I must talk to the Alachua chief. If he can give me food, I must get it to the fort."

"He will be glad to trade," said Has-se. "Let us speak to him."

René got out his bundle. Together they went to the Alachua chief.

"My brother, the young white chief, needs corn for his people," said Has-se. "He has brought things to trade."

"We are glad to trade," said the Alachua chief. "We have much corn. What has the young white chief brought?"

René opened his bundle. The chief's eyes opened in wonder. To him it was a wonderful treasure. There were knives, hatchets, mirrors, and fish hooks.

"My people traded with Micco for corn. Then Chitta, our enemy, burned the store house. My people need food," said René.

"Let the white chief say what he wants."

"Twelve canoes full of corn. Send with me enough warriors to bring the corn safely home."

"And these things are mine?"

"They are yours. My uncle is chief of the fort. In his name I make a promise. Such a bundle we will give for each canoe full of corn. Your warriors will be treated well. When the corn is in the fort, the warriors may come back."

"It is a good trade," said the chief. "Give me a day. I will speak to our wise men."

After a day the chief sent word he would make the trade. The Indians began to load the canoes. There was no trouble getting the warriors to go. All who had not seen the fort wanted to go. They wanted to see the great "thunder bows"—the cannon.

Chapter 18. RENÉ TO THE RESCUE

And so, two weeks after he came, René was ready to go. Has-se was to go along. Eagle, Has-se's brother-in-law, was to lead fifty Alachua warriors.

René liked the Indians. Sadly he said good-bye to his friends, Day Star, Micco, and the Alachua chief. Many others came to say good-bye.

The twenty canoes started out next morning. Twelve were loaded with corn, eight with warriors. Micco's people and the Alachuas came to see them off. René, Has-se, Eagle, and a young warrior named Bear's Paw were in the first canoe. As it shot from the bank, the Indians shouted:

"Good-bye, Ta-lah-lo-ko!" they called out to René.
"Good-bye to the young white chief!"
"Do not forget us, Ta-lah-lo-ko."

They got through the great swamp safely. But then the warriors began to watch carefully. Many men, they could see, had gone this way shortly before. Sharp Indian eyes searched the trees and bushes. They sent two scouts ahead. They soon came back. Dead camp fire ashes showed a war party was not far ahead. No one asked who they could be. Everybody knew. The outlaw Seminoles were on the war path.

René was uneasy. He knew Chitta had joined the Seminoles. Chitta knew the fort was weak. Chitta would tell the Seminoles. The Seminoles would surely attack the fort.

René had guessed the truth. Only a day before, Chitta, Cat-sha, and the Seminoles had passed. Cat-sha had called his band together to attack the fort. They meant to surround the fort first. Then they hoped to cut down anybody who got outside. When they had killed enough, they wanted to storm the fort.

But the Seminoles found other Indians there before them. A strong war party of southern Indians was hidden in the forest. They had followed the whites who had burned their village. These Indians were watching their chance. Both war parties wanted to take the fort. Both hated the white men. Cat-sha talked with the other chief. He was willing to work together. Cat-sha was well known as a bold fighter and leader. So Cat-sha was to lead both bands.

They made their attack. The white men's cannon finally drove them back. Then Cat-sha planned to get the white soldiers outside. Because Simon was so foolish, the Indians almost got them all. Cat-sha had hidden his men cleverly. He would have wiped out the colony. Only the sudden attack on the Indians saved Fort Caroline.

When René found out the Seminoles were on the war path, he pushed ahead fast. Eagle passed the word to his warriors. They were eager to catch the hated Seminoles, too. The canoes picked up speed. They went so fast they soon heard the thunder of guns. The battle had just begun.

René and his friends landed below the fort. A few warriors stayed to guard the canoes. The others crept up the river bank. Here they hid themselves. Scouts went ahead to see how things were. Two hours later they came back. They told how Cat-sha had hidden his men. Even as they talked, Simon's men were marching out.

Eagle ordered the warriors to move ahead. René

and Has-se were in the front line. They came to the battlefield just as the whites were going down.

Eagle gave the war cry. The warriors rushed forward. The Seminoles were too surprised to fight. Eagle's men scattered them left and right. Charging the Seminoles, it was René who shouted, "France to the rescue! France to the rescue!"

Chapter 19. THE SECRET TUNNEL

The Seminoles and other Indians had scattered in the forest. René and his friends knew they would soon be back. They knew, too, that only the surprise had driven them off. The enemy had many men. René and Has-se had fifty. Soon the Seminole scouts would be back. Cat-sha would rally his men and attack. Eagle, too, knew this. He wanted to bring in the corn and leave.

So Eagle and his men hurried up the river to the fort. But now they did not know what to do. If they went to the gate, the guards would shoot. The white men did not know who had saved them. When the guards started to shoot, the Seminoles would hear. When they did, they would attack. Eagle called his men together to talk it over.

While they talked, Has-se took René aside. In a whisper he said:

"Ta-lah-lo-ko, the time has come. You remember that I escaped from the fort. I did not tell you how. It is my people's secret. You have fought and bled for me. You are my brother. I have given you the flamingo feather. Now I can tell you. First you must promise never to tell the secret. You must not tell your own people."

"I promise, Has-se."

"All right. You know my people helped build the fort. When we did, we built a secret tunnel. Micco ordered it so. It runs under a wall. He thought some day we might need it. If we were outside, we could get in. If we were locked in, we could get out. This is how I got out when your people locked me in. I got out the guard house window easily. Once out, I was free. I escaped to the bank of the river through the tunnel."

René was surprised to hear this.

"A tunnel!" he said. "That could be a great danger. Do all your people know about it, Has-se?"

"No," said Has-se. "No more than twenty know it. They will never tell. They have promised Micco. They would die before they told. You are the only other one who knows about it."

"Well," said René, "if it's there we should use it.

Show it to me. I will get into the fort. Then I can go see my uncle. I shall tell him we are here with food. You and the others go to the river gate. I'll get the gate open. You can bring in the corn and get your pay. Then you will be able to leave. Eagle and his warriors want to get back."

"Good!" said Has-se.

"Oh, Has-se," cried René. "I am sorry to have you go. You have been a brother to me."

Has-se took his hand.

"I, too, am sorry," he said. "You will always be my white brother."

Then the two went back to Eagle.

"My brother," said Has-se, "René can get to his people. He knows a way. Let us go alone. I will soon be back."

"Go," said Eagle.

The boys took a canoe and quietly paddled to the fort. One part of the fort was near the river bank. Has-se watched the bank. Suddenly he stopped the canoe. He reached up and pulled some bushes aside. Now he lifted aside a big flat strip of bark. A small hole was in the bank. They tied the canoe, and Has-se crawled in. René followed. Everything was black, but there was only one way to go. It seemed to René that they crawled a full mile. It must have been about a hundred yards.

At last Has-se stopped. He reached up and raised another piece of bark.

"René," he whispered.

"Yes."

"Listen! We are under your uncle's house. Crawl over me. Watch your head."

René crawled over Has-se's body. He scrambled out of the tunnel. He reached back and felt for Has-se's hand. He gave it a squeeze.

"Good-bye," he whispered.

"Good-bye, Ta-lah-lo-ko," whispered Has-se. In a moment he was gone.

Chapter 20. FOOD FOR THE FORT

René found himself in darkness. He raised himself and banged his head. The house was set on stones about two feet above the ground. He had hit his head against the floor. He felt for the bark strip and put it back over the tunnel. Now he crawled toward the end of the house.

René stood up. Everything was quiet in the fort yard. He looked around, saw no light. Then he turned toward his uncle's house, just behind him. A faint light came through the shutters. There was no guard before his uncle's house. René wondered what could be wrong. He looked toward the great gate. There were no guards there. He listened a moment longer. Still he heard nothing. He tapped softly on the window. Nothing happened. He tapped again—a little louder. Some one moved a chair inside. René tapped a third time. The window opened softly.

"Who is there? Who goes there?" said a voice.

René knew it. It was Le Moyne, his old teacher.

Still René said nothing. He tapped on the shutter. The light went out. Softly the shutter opened. Le Moyne looked out.

"Who is there? What do you want?" he asked.

"Sh!" said René. "It is I—René. Say no more. Go to the door and let me in. I must see my uncle. I have good news."

"René!" cried Le Moyne. "Come in!" He opened the shutter and helped René in through the window. When he had him inside he threw his arms around him and kissed him. Then he said:

"Lad, we thought you were dead. Your uncle has been very sick. He is still weak. Let us be careful. I'll tell him you are here. Let me break the good news gently, though. We must keep him as quiet as we can."

Le Moyne went into Laudonnière's room. René followed him closely and stayed at the door.

"My captain," said Le Moyne, shaking him, "awake. I have news for you—news from the dead."

"Come, come," said the old man. "What is the matter? Have you been dreaming?"

"No, this is no dream. This is real."

"What is?"

"One whom you love. One you thought dead."

"What?" cried the old man, sitting up. "One I thought dead? You mean René—my son? Where is he? Where is he?"

"Here I am, uncle," cried René. He ran to him and threw his arms around him. The old man held him tight. Tears shone in his eyes.

"My boy, my boy," he said over and over.

René quickly told his story.

"And so," he said, "I have the corn. Twelve canoe loads are outside. We must let them in and pay the Indians. They want to go back tonight."

"Ah, René," said the old man, "I am no longer leader here. While I was sick, Simon made himself captain. He does as he wishes. The men follow him. You must go to him. He will pay your friends. The men are starving. He will give anything for food."

"Simon is captain!" cried René. "I cannot believe it."

"It is true, boy. Go now. Tell him your story. Get the corn and come back quickly."

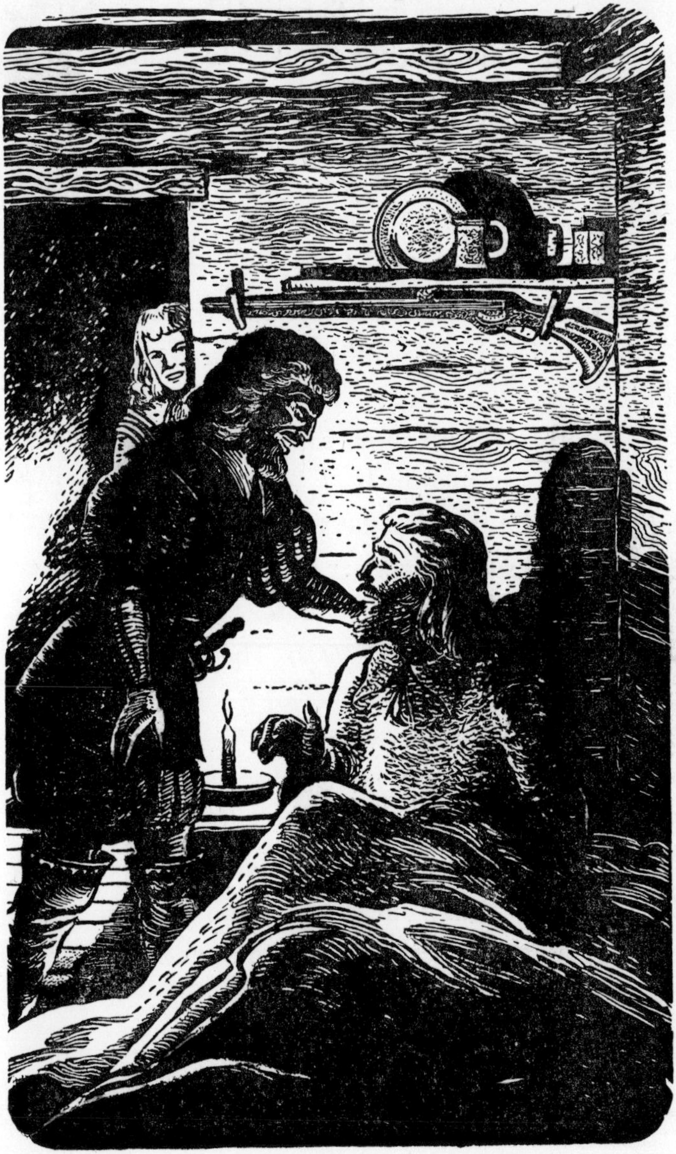

René went out to find Simon. When he did, the old soldier could hardly speak. He thought René had come back from the dead.

"Come, come, Simon! Wake up. I tell you I have food outside. We must let my Indian friends in," cried René.

"But how did you get back?"

"Never mind that. Can't you understand? There is food, FOOD! If you want to boss the fort, do something."

"To tell the truth, boy, I'm sick of it all. If your uncle will only take us back home, he shall be captain again. I'll do what he says any way."

"Well, he says to take the corn."

"All right. We need it badly enough. We can pay your Indians, too, if he says so. They will not attack us?"

"No, no! They are my friends. You fool, did they not save your life? Who was it who attacked the Seminoles?"

"What? You mean it? Was it you who saved us? Heaven bless you! Your friends shall be mine. They did a good day's work. Was it you cried, 'France to the rescue'?"

"It was."

"You are a brave boy. We are proud of you."

Simon led the way to the river gate. He called

out the guard to help. At the gate Has-se and the others were waiting. The white men were glad to see the corn. The fort was really in a bad way.

Simon ordered the men to put the corn into the store house. René and Le Moyne packed the twelve bundles for the Indians. René made up another bundle for Has-se and one for his sister. Eagle, too, got his share of knives and hatchets.

René took the Indian warriors around the fort. He showed them the great "thunder bows"—the cannon.

It was past midnight when the Indians left. René and Has-se sadly said good-bye once more. Both feared they might never meet again.

One by one the Indian canoes slipped away. René watched the last one go. He went to his own room and fell into bed. Worn out, he was asleep when his head hit the pillow.

Chapter 21. THE COLONY GIVES UP

It was late when René awoke. He could hardly believe he was back home. He jumped up, dressed, and ate a quick breakfast. Then he went to see his uncle.

His uncle was feeling much stronger and better.

He was sitting up the first time in weeks. He sat in a big chair near the window, waiting for René. When René came in, the old man took his hand.

"My boy," he said, "I can not tell you how glad I am to see you. Now tell me where you have been."

René told him the whole story. He told how he and Has-se had followed Chitta and Cat-sha. His uncle listened eagerly. The boy told how he had been wounded and how he had got the corn. His uncle then told what had happened at the fort.

At last both finished their stories.

"You have been a man, René," said Laudonnière. "I am proud of you. You got the food for us. I will not say much about how you left. I must warn you, though. I was your captain here. You were my soldier. You did leave without asking me. That was not right. A good soldier takes orders. You must always remember this."

"I know, uncle," said René. "That was wrong. I will remember. You will not have any more trouble from me."

"Well, we will not starve yet, thanks to you. But the men want to leave."

"Uncle, I cannot believe it. They gave their word they would stay. What will the King say?"

"I can do no more, my boy. I am captain no longer. Simon is now their leader."

"May I talk to him? Maybe I could make him see they are wrong."

"You can try. I do not think they will listen."

René did go to Simon.

"Simon," said René, "how can you do this? You promised the King you would stay. Ribault will come with more men and food."

"It's no use, René," said Simon. "It's too late. This is no land for white men. There is fever here. There is no food. If we stay, we starve. At least we can die in France. Our ship is ready. We can use the food you brought to get us home. We do not dare leave the fort. The forest is full of Indians waiting to kill us. If we stay, we die like rats in a trap. You may as well make the best of it. Help us get ready."

"No. If you want to go, we can not stop you. We can not hold the fort alone. We will have to come along. I will get my uncle ready," said René.

René's uncle was still not strong. René packed his things for him. Laudonnière had important papers which had to go.

The men got their new boat into the river. René shook his head when he saw it. Nobody with common sense would try to sail the ocean with it. But in two more weeks the men had it ready. Another week and they got the food on board. Nothing was left in Fort Caroline except the big cannon.

One fine morning they all marched on board. René and Le Moyne carried Laudonnière. He did not want to go, but he could do nothing else. The sails filled and the boat sailed down the river. The little colony had started bravely, with high hopes. Now they had given up. They hoped never to see the New World again. Even their crazy little ship, they thought, was safer.

The Indians shot a few arrows at them. They stood on the river bank and angrily watched them go.

That day they got to the mouth of the river. The ocean was booming loud against the sand bar. The water was too rough. The little ship dropped anchor to await better weather.

Chapter 22. HELP COMES

While they waited, the men tried to make the ship stronger. They had put moss and pitch in the cracks. Already the ship was leaking badly. The pumps had to be worked day and night to keep her floating.

René's uncle knew the ship could never make it. He and René were in a bad spot. To go meant death on the ocean. To stay meant death by the Seminoles.

"We may as well die with them," said Laudonnière.

They waited a few days more. Then the great waves went down. The wind blew right. The sailors raised the sails. The crazy little ship got over the sand bar and headed out to sea. The men happily waved good-bye to the shore.

But they did not get far. Just as the land grew dim, the lookout cried, "A sail! A sail!" All eyes looked to the south. A white speck showed far away.

"What is it? French?"

"No, Spanish."

"Then we shall all be killed!"

"No, no! It is Ribault coming to help us."

All stood at the rail, straining their eyes to see. Soon they saw a second sail, then a third. At last a whole fleet bore down on them. They swept swiftly closer and closer. Their own little ship was leaking again. They could never hope to get away if the ships were the enemy. Nor could they fight. The smallest ship coming had more guns and men than they. All they could do was hope they were friends.

Le Moyne and René had carried Laudonnière on deck. He lay on a cot, looking at the ships. At last he shook his head.

"They are not French," he said.

The others groaned. If not French, they must be

Spanish. But then they saw the first ship's flag. It was not Spain's yellow flag, but England's red one. The men shouted happily. They jumped and danced on the deck. Someone ran to get their own flag. A moment later the lily flag of France flew in the breeze. The English ships stopped close by.

Bold Sir John Hawkins, the famous sea dog, it was, in command. No Spanish ship was safe when Hawkins sailed. But France and England were friendly. Hawkins was going back home. He had been sailing the Spanish Main. He had taken many Spanish ships. Hawkins waited until they were loaded with gold and silver from Mexico and Peru. Then he took their gold and silver.

When Hawkins saw the French ship, he laughed.

"You will never get home in that tub," he said. "I will give you a ship. Have you food? Not enough? I will give you some."

He did. He gave them the ship and enough food to get home on. Laudonnière again took command. In the name of King Charles IX of France he thanked the English. Hawkins turned his ships and set sail again.

The French now sailed back to the River of May. They had to move the food to the new ship. So at sunset they were back where they had started.

Laudonnière tried again to get them to stay. They

were willing to have him lead them back, but they would not stay. There were too many against him. He had to agree. The men started to move their things to the new ship.

But when they finished, the weather had turned bad again. For a week the waves roared against the sand bar. Late one afternoon some one saw ships coming. They were headed for Fort Caroline. Again there was great excitement. Were they French? English? Spanish? The next day would bring the answer.

Everyone was out bright and early. The sun lighted up seven tall ships outside the sand bar. All seven flew the lily flag of France. Then they did shout and cheer! It must be Ribault, with food and more people. Now no one talked about going back home. Now the cry was, "Ho, for Fort Caroline! Death to the Seminoles!"

Crowding on the sail, they sailed out to meet Ribault. The flags flew and the cannon roared a welcome. It was Ribault, as they had guessed. Laudonnière, helped by René, came on board Ribault's own ship.

Ribault was angry to hear the men had overthrown his good friend Laudonnière.

"I'll hang them!" he cried. "Get a new leader, will they? We shall see. Who are they?"

"No, Jean," said Laudonnière. "We are not going

to punish them. They have had a hard time. They are hungry. Many have been killed by Indians. It is a new, strange land to them. Let us forget about it."

"Well," said Ribault at last, "have it your way. I still think we should punish them."

Laudonnière told Ribault the whole story. He was proud to tell what René had done. Ribault asked to see the boy.

"You are a brave lad," he said. "You saved the colony for France. You are an honor to your uncle. I wish I could reward you. I shall never forget what you have done. The King himself shall hear of this."

René blushed and said little. But he was sure he could fight the Seminoles alone now. The rest of the day he was the happiest boy in the world.

Chapter 23. THE SPANISH COME

All but one of Ribault's ships were too heavy to cross the sand bar. This one and Laudonnière's English ship had to carry the people and the food to Fort Caroline. The work took many days. There were three hundred new people. They had brought food, guns, and tools. They had to carry everything over the sand bar and up the river.

The new people were not very happy when they saw the fort. Nothing was left but a few Indians who were taking what could be found. They ran off when the white men came back. The cannon were pulled down. There were not enough houses.

René was happy to be back. He said to himself, "Soon Micco's people will come back. Then I shall see Has-se again. Maybe he will go to France with me some day."

But again there was trouble ahead. The men got to work quickly, making the fort stronger and building homes. But as they worked, a strong, cruel enemy was on the way. The King of Spain had sent his men to take the land called Florida. When he said Florida, he meant all the land up to Virginia. For him there was no western end to Florida. The Spaniards had come there first, he said. The land belonged to Spain. Proud King Philip would have no French there. And so he sent Don Pedro Menendez with ships and men to hold the country. Don Pedro had a mighty fleet—thirty-four ships. Three thousand soldiers were on those ships. Don Pedro was going to build a fort and start a city. But Don Pedro had another job first. He was going to run every Frenchman out of Florida.

Soon after Ribault had come, the great Spanish fleet got there. Sailing north, they saw the French ships near the River of May. Ship after ship slipped up the coast. Don Pedro's flag ship pulled close. The great Don Pedro himself came to the rail. Ribault was at the rail of his flag ship also.

"Where are these ships from?" called Don Pedro.

"From France," said Ribault.

"What are you doing here?"

"We bring people and food to Fort Caroline."

"Fort Caroline?"

"It is the fort built for King Charles of France. This is a French colony."

"And why are the French on Spanish land?"

"And who wants to know?"

"I am Don Pedro of Spain. This is my fleet. I sail for King Philip of Spain. I am here to hold Florida for him. We have orders to kill on sea or land. I spare nobody. When the sun rises, I am coming. I shall take your ships. I shall kill anybody on board."

But Ribault and the French did not scare easily. Ribault threw back his head and laughed.

"Ha!" he cried. "Why wait until morning, great bag of wind? Why do you not kill us now?"

"I will!" roared Don Pedro. "Cut loose, captains! Kill these French dogs!"

Night had already come by now, but Don Pedro was out of his senses. He shouted, screamed, and ran around like a mad man. His captains cut their ships loose and bore down on Ribault's six ships.

But Ribault was ready. Before the Spanish could reach him, his ships, too, had cut loose. The sails went up and out they went to sea. The Spaniards chased them the rest of the night. Ribault was a good sailor and the night was dark. By daylight he was gone. The Spanish ships came back to the River of May.

"We will mop up this fort," said Don Pedro.

But Laudonnière had not been sleeping, either. During the night his men dragged the heavy cannon to the mouth of the river. His men were ready on both banks. Just inside the sand bar were the other two ships. Their guns pointed at the river mouth. His plan was simple. The Spanish ships would have to cross the bar one by one. As one came over, he would blast it with the ship's guns. If it got by, the land cannon could hardly miss at the river.

Don Pedro did not like the looks of things. Angry as he was, he had sense enough to hold back. He did not even try to land his soldiers. He now ordered his captains to sail south. Miles down the coast he could get over the bar. So he sailed to the Indian village where René and his uncle had first landed.

"We can wait," he said. "Here we will build our fort. Here we will start a great Spanish city. When I am ready, I will wipe out these French."

The Spaniards poured out of the ships. Don Pedro himself led a great parade on land. He even made a speech. Then he claimed the land for the King of Spain. As he did, the Spanish cannon boomed. The soldiers shouted and sang. Then they rushed forward and tore down the Indian village.

The poor Indians who watched could not understand. The white men they knew were French. The Spaniards they did not know. It did not take them long to learn. The Spanish soldiers now rushed at them. Most Indians they killed in cold blood. The ones who lived were made slaves. They put them to work building their fort for them.

Don Pedro was pleased. On the smoking, bloodstained ground he laid out his new city. He gave it its name—St. Augustine. And St. Augustine it is to this day. It is said to be the oldest city in the United States.

The poor Indian chief tried to get the Spaniards to stop. He begged Don Pedro to spare his village, not to kill his people. Nobody listened to him.

"Kill that barking dog!" cried Don Pedro. But the chief slipped into the woods before they could get him. He gathered a few picked warriors together. The next day they got safely to Fort Caroline.

They had a hard time getting in. Since the Seminole attack, the French were afraid of Indians.

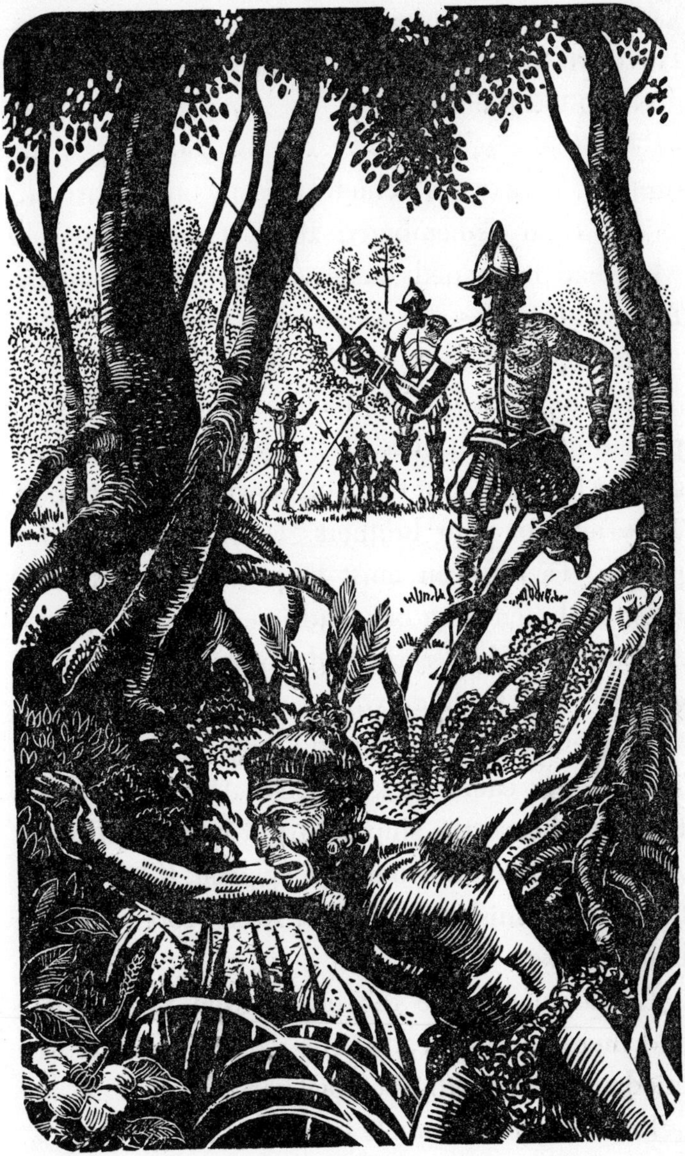

Luckily, René was near the gate when they came. He heard the guard tell them to wait. He looked out and spotted the chief.

"Let them in," he said. "I know them. They are friendly. That one is a chief. He is my uncle's friend."

The chief remembered René. Quickly he told what had happened. René took him to his uncle. Laudonnière was still weak and stayed in his room.

The poor old chief told his story again.

"Ta-lah," he said, "you have been my friend. Your people have been good to my people. The French are our brothers. But these other white men are bad. They are not your brothers. They have killed my people. Ta-lah, you must help us. Help us drive these bad men from our land."

"You are right," said Laudonnière. "They are our enemies, too. I will do what I can."

Laudonnière sent a man to Ribault with the news. The answer came back quickly. All soldiers were to get on board the ships. Ribault had a bold plan. He would swoop down on the Spanish. If he waited, they would finish their fort. A strong fort would be hard to take.

Laudonnière gave the order. Men rushed here and there, getting ready. The women and children cried and screamed. The dogs barked.

René begged his uncle to let him go.

"No, my boy," said the old man. "This is a job for soldiers. You are brave and strong, but you are only a boy. You stay with me. I am too weak to go. I need help here, too."

So the fighting men marched away to join the fleet. Only the old, the sick, the women, and the children were left. Le Moyne stayed to help care for Laudonnière. Old Simon, too, had to stay. He was captain of the guard.

Chapter 24. DON PEDRO ATTACKS

After landing Don Pedro and his men, the Spanish fleet sailed back to Spain. Only a few small ships stayed. They got inside the sand bar. So Ribault seemed to have a good chance. He had six ships. He had a fair number of soldiers. The French were sure they could wipe out St. Augustine before their fort was built.

When Ribault got there, the tide was low. He could not get his ships over the sand bar. They waited for the tide to rise. By this time the Spaniards had seen them. They knew why Ribault was there. Quickly they got ready for the attack.

But then, without warning, a terrible blast of

wind hit the ships. Another and another followed. The men had never seen such a storm before. The French ships fought the great waves as well as they could. They were lucky to stay afloat. Don Pedro smiled as he watched them.

"The storm drives them down the coast," he said. "They can never live through it. The waves will smash them. Come, men, this is our chance! Their soldiers are on the ships. No one is left to defend their Fort Caroline. We will get them out of Florida. Ha! Laugh at Don Pedro, will they?"

Don Pedro picked five hundred men to go. The storm raged for three days. Beaten by the wind and rain, he pushed through swamps and forests. He had taken some Indians along as guides. When they did not reach Fort Caroline quickly, he thought they were tricking him.

"Kill them," he ordered cruelly. "And make it hurt. We will find our own way."

At last they reached the River of May. They followed the river until they came to the high hill. They looked down at the fort. A few lights were burning.

The French in the fort were worried about the storm. They knew the ships could not ride through it. Already they had begun to fear the ships were lost.

Old Simon was captain of the guards. René and the old men had been working under him. The boy had done his work well. Each night he took his cross bow and walked along the walls. The wind and rain made it a nasty job, but René was glad to do it. He was doing a soldier's work. He never complained. The others grumbled about it.

"Why must we soak ourselves every night?" said one. "The Spaniards are gone. The Indians are gone. Who would attack us? Who would come in such a storm?"

Morning of the fourth night of storm came. René was just finishing his turn. For two hours he had marched in the cold rain. The next guard came at last to take his place. Cold and tired, René went to his uncle's house. He was so tired he did not even take off his wet clothes. He threw himself down. In a moment he was sound asleep.

The soldier who took René's place was tired, too. He walked the wall a few times. As usual, he saw or heard nothing to worry him. He slipped into a dry corner nearby. In a few minutes he was snoring.

While he slept, the Spaniards got up to the back gate. Don Pedro gave the signal. Five hundred Spanish soldiers came pouring into the fort.

The sleeping guard awoke. A Spaniard hacked at him with his sword. The guard gave a last scream as he fell. The Spaniards now rushed the houses, yelling and shouting.

René sprang to the door. He threw it open and stopped. For a moment he could not move. Flames burst from the tents and houses. The fort was bright as day. He saw old men, women, and children running and screaming. Most of them were in their night clothes. Wherever they turned, they met Spaniards. A soldier swung his sword at an old man. Badly cut, the old man turned to get away. He ran straight into a Spanish spear. The point broke out through his back. He sagged to the ground. The soldiers laughed. René saw a woman running, carrying a child. A big soldier leaped after her, buried his dagger in her back. The wind still howled, but the screams rose above the wind.

René saw all this in a moment. Then he remembered his uncle. He slammed the door and ran to his uncle's room. The old man was pale but very calm. When he heard the first scream, he guessed what had happened. Still too weak to help himself, he had Le Moyne get him into his armor. The old man knew he would be killed, but he meant to go down fighting.

"Uncle!" cried René. "Come on. There is no time to lose. The fort is full of Spaniards. We haven't got a chance to fight. Follow me and save your life. I know a way to get out."

René had just remembered the tunnel.

The two men followed him outside. To their surprise he led them under the house. They were not a moment too soon. The Spaniards had just found out where Laudonnière lived. The three heard them burst into the house. They stormed from room to room, looking for the French leader. They threw the furniture around and kicked the doors open.

René crawled ahead in the dark, feeling for the bark strip. Le Moyne came next. Laudonnière pulled himself along after them.

"Follow me," whispered René. He slipped into the tunnel. The other two followed. They came out on the river bank. No one was around.

René's uncle was amazed by what he had seen.

"Who made this tunnel?" he asked. "And, René, how did you know about it?"

But René had promised Has-se never to tell.

"Uncle," he said, "let's not talk about it now. You are still in great danger. Let's get you away first. We can talk about it some other time. Now you and Le Moyne can get to the mouth of the river. Our two ships are still there. I'll go back. Maybe I can save a few of our people. I will not be long. I can catch up with you soon."

"No, René. Come with me. You may be killed," cried the old man.

"Uncle, I must try to help."

"I guess you are right, boy. I love you too much. Go, do what you can. Take no chances. Follow us when you can. I will see you soon, I hope."

René's uncle was wrong. It would be long before he saw René again.

Chapter 25. CAPTURED

René made his way back through the tunnel. Carefully he climbed out. He crawled to the end of the house to watch and listen. He had been there only a minute when he heard someone groan. Listening carefully, he heard it again. Whoever it was was close by. Surely, thought René, it must be a Frenchman. He began to crawl toward the sound. Then he heard it a third time. It was so close, René almost jumped up. Softly he whispered:

"Who is there? I am René."

"René!" came a weak whisper. "It is I, your old friend Simon. I am badly hurt. I cannot get away. The Spanish devils will find me by daylight."

"Cheer up, Simon," said René. "If you can walk or crawl, I can save you. Where are you hurt?"

"I can crawl or walk," said Simon. "If you have any way to get out, tell me. I am ready to give up."

So René led Simon to the tunnel. The old man followed with many stops and groans. At last they came out at the river bank.

"Go now," said René. "You can make it to the ships. My uncle and Le Moyne are on the way. If you make it, you will be safe. I'll go back and try to help others."

Once more René crawled back. Again he watched and listened, hoping to help his people. The Spaniards were still shouting and hunting the French. Now and then a cry or scream came. The Spaniards were finding those who had been hiding. When they found somebody, they killed him.

Suddenly another house nearby broke into flames. René pulled back into the shadow. As he did, he saw a pile of books and papers lying near the house. He needed only one look to know them. They were his uncle's. The Spaniards had thrown them out the window.

René knew his uncle would like to have them. There seemed to be no more people he could help. He made up his mind to save the papers. It was a dangerous thing to do. He had to leave the building and come out into the open. The brave boy slipped quickly out and picked up an armful of books. He made another trip, then another. Each time he piled his load into the tunnel.

He had got almost all when the sun arose. One more trip and he would have them all. The light made this last trip even more risky. Was it worth the chance? René thought it was. Just as he picked the papers up, someone shouted. René looked up. Two Spaniards were rushing him with swords. They looked like giants.

René thought fast. If he ran for the tunnel, they would find the papers. Still holding the papers, he ran into the house. He slammed the door and ran down the big hall. A window was open at the end. He dived through it just as the soldiers got to the door. He could hear them slamming doors and shouting. They thought he was hiding.

René scrambled under the building again. He got into the tunnel and closed the opening. The last load of paper he put with the others. Then he moved them all to the middle of the tunnel. He also brought along a small, locked iron box. This he carefully buried deep in the wall.

While he was doing this, the Spaniards were getting more and more puzzled. They went through every room again. They could not find him nor the papers he had carried.

Finally one said, "There must be a secret room. Let us speak to Don Pedro."

"Burn the building," said Don Pedro.

They stood and watched it burn to the ground.

"That settles that," said Don Pedro.

The soldiers were still puzzled, though. One shook his head.

"That's strange," he said. "He did not even try to run. Just let himself be burned up."

"Yes," said the other. "He did not even cry out."

"Well, we got him. No use worrying about him."

They went on then to look for others.

René now crawled to the end of the tunnel again. He put the cover back and pulled the vines over it. Then he began to work his way slowly along the bank. It was now broad daylight. Sometimes he crawled in the bushes. Now and then he waded in the river.

After several hours he came to the high hill overlooking the fort. He was now worn out. He climbed to the top and looked around. Sadly he saw the yellow flag of Spain flying from the fort. At the river mouth lay the two small French ships. They were his only hope. He wanted to try to get to them then, but he was too tired. He threw himself down in the bushes. He wanted an hour's sleep before he tried to get to the ships. He lay about where Chitta had lain when Cat-sha found him. In a moment he was sound asleep.

René dreamed again what he had seen at the fort.

He rolled and groaned in his sleep. Had he been awake, he would have seen an Indian band making their way along the river. He would have known their chief from far off. He was the giant Cat-sha, leading his Seminole braves. With him was Chitta the Snake. Three prisoners walked behind them. Two were Frenchmen. The third was an Indian boy who had got away from the Spaniards. The three had jumped from the walls of the fort when Don Pedro attacked. They had got safely into the forest.

There they had met the Seminoles. Cat-sha and a few braves had stayed to catch careless Frenchmen. The Seminoles were planning a great feast. Cat-sha wanted a few enemies to burn at the stake. Most of his Seminoles had already gone back to the swamp. Cat-sha was now following with his prisoners. The Seminole canoes were hidden on the other side of the hill.

Sending his braves on, Cat-sha climbed the hill with Chitta. Cat-sha wanted to have a last look around. As they came to the top they heard René groan. Quietly they crept to where he lay. The two Indians looked at each other and grinned. The young white chief! Here was a prize to take back. In another minute René awoke to find himself tied hand and foot. He looked up. He stared into the eyes of his cruel and bitter enemies.

Chapter 26. THE SEMINOLE VILLAGE

There was a sneering smile on Chitta's face. René looked at Cat-sha. A cruel, cold look met him there, too. Chitta was thinking of the wrestling match. Now he had his chance to get even. Cat-sha knew René had led the Alachuas against the Seminoles. Cat-sha would be only too happy to wipe out an enemy.

They loosened the ropes around his ankles so he could walk. The three now joined the others at the river. The other Seminoles were glad to see another prisoner. They searched him and took what they wanted. Then they tied him up again and threw him flat into a canoe. René got a look at the other prisoners but could not talk to them.

The Seminoles wanted to keep René well and strong. A weak prisoner would die too quickly at the stake. So they gave him plenty of food and water. At first René was not going to eat or drink. That would bring the end on faster. He soon gave up the idea. That would mean giving up. He made up his mind to watch his chance to get away. So he ate everything they gave him.

René had not had enough sleep for a long time. He had no chance to get away now, so he tried to sleep as much as he could. The Indians looked at him in surprise. They thought he would beg for mercy. Instead, he just went to sleep.

They stayed where they were that day. That night they started for the great Okefenokee Swamp—the Seminoles' home. They paddled silently past the French ships. No one saw them, and in a few minutes they were safely past. René passed so close his uncle could have called to him. But neither René nor his uncle knew that.

René lay flat in the canoe. He could not tell where they were going. He did not know they were making the same trip he and Has-se had made. He had no chance to talk to the other prisoners. The Seminoles had each one in a different canoe. At night they tied them to trees far apart.

Day after day René watched the Seminoles' faces. Only one gave him any hope. This one was a boy about his own age. René soon found out he was the Indian Cat-sha had captured. When the Seminoles caught René, they had three white prisoners. So Cat-sha asked the Indian boy if he wanted to save himself. There was one way he could—by joining the Seminoles. This young Indian, E-chee, the Deer, said he would.

But E-chee did not intend ever to join the Seminoles. He, too, watched his chances. He meant to escape when he could.

E-chee remembered René well. He was careful not to give any sign that he did. When no one was watching he looked at René to let him know he was a friend. When E-chee guarded the prisoners, he was as cruel as the Seminoles. He knew Cat-sha did not yet trust him. When Cat-sha was watching, he kicked the white prisoners. Cat-sha would smile.

"You will make a good Seminole some day," he would say.

At last E-chee had a chance to talk to René. They had come to the great swamp. By now René guessed where they were. One dark night E-chee was on guard. The other Seminoles were asleep. E-chee quietly came to René.

"Ta-lah-lo-ko," he whispered.

René had fallen asleep, but he awoke.

In a moment the whisper came again.

"Ta-lah-lo-ko."

"Who are you?" whispered René.

"I am E-chee. I saw you when you and your uncle first came. Do you remember the Indian village where you first stopped?"

"Are you not E-chee the Seminole?"

"They think I am. Cat-sha said they would spare

me if I became a Seminole. I said I would. I am waiting a chance to get away."

"Do you think you can?" asked René.

"I do not know. I can try. I would rather die than be a Seminole."

"Do you know where we are?"

"This is the great swamp called Okefenokee."

"I thought so," said René. "What does Cat-sha plan to do?"

"Tomorrow we leave the canoes. We go by a secret path. The path takes us to the Seminole village. There the Seminoles will have a big feast. They will burn you and the others at the stake."

"Listen!" said René. "Can you find the land of the Alachuas?"

"Yes," said E-chee.

"Reach into my coat. Feel in the lining."

E-chee did. He pulled out the flamingo feather on the gold chain.

"Guard it with your life," said René. "If you escape, take it to the Alachuas. Ask first for Chief Micco. Then find his son, Has-se. Tell him what has happened to me. Give him the flamingo feather. Ask him to send help."

Just as he finished, a twig snapped. E-chee jumped up and kicked René.

"Dog!" he cried. "Take that!"

René thought he had been tricked. But then he heard Cat-sha's voice.

"Why are you kicking him, E-chee?" he asked.

"This is the worst one," said E-chee. "I caught him trying to get loose. I just tied him up again."

"Good," said Cat-sha. "You will make a good warrior some day, E-chee. It pleases me that you are watching."

Cat-sha went on to look at the other prisoners.

"Don't give up hope," whispered E-chee. Then he, too, was gone.

The next day the Seminoles ran the canoes ashore. René got up and stepped on land. He saw at once where they were. Here the snake had bitten him.

The Seminoles hid their canoes in the vines. Now they started down the path in single file. René hoped E-chee would watch the way carefully.

They got to the Seminole village that night. Everybody ran out to meet them. When the Indians saw the prisoners, they shouted for joy. They had all heard of René, the young white chief. The squaws and children crowded around him, screaming, pulling his hair, pushing him. René took it all quietly. If he got angry they would only get worse, he knew. He knew they wanted him to lose his temper.

At last he could stand it no longer. A big ugly lad, taller than René, had joined the others. He began jabbing René with a sharp knife. When he did, he pushed his face close and laughed. René's hands were tied together. He stepped back, raised both fists together, and smashed the boy in the face. The Indian hit the ground.

The other Indians screamed and shouted. The boy jumped up and tried to plunge his knife into René's heart. But now the warriors stepped up. They pushed the Indian boy aside. Then they led René to a little hut. Here they tied his ankles so he could not stand. They closed the door and left him alone.

The Seminole village was an island higher than the swamp. Here they raised corn and pumpkins. There were about a hundred huts in the village. The Seminoles had about five hundred people in all. About two hundred were warriors.

On all sides stretched the great swamp. There was only one way to the island—the path. The Seminoles kept a warrior on guard there day and night. Nobody could surprise them. Enemies would have to come one at a time. It was just as hard to get away as it was to get to.

The very night Cat-sha got back, a strange thing happened. The warrior guarding the path heard some one singing. It was an Indian death song. The voice came from the bushes nearby.

Then came a loud cry:

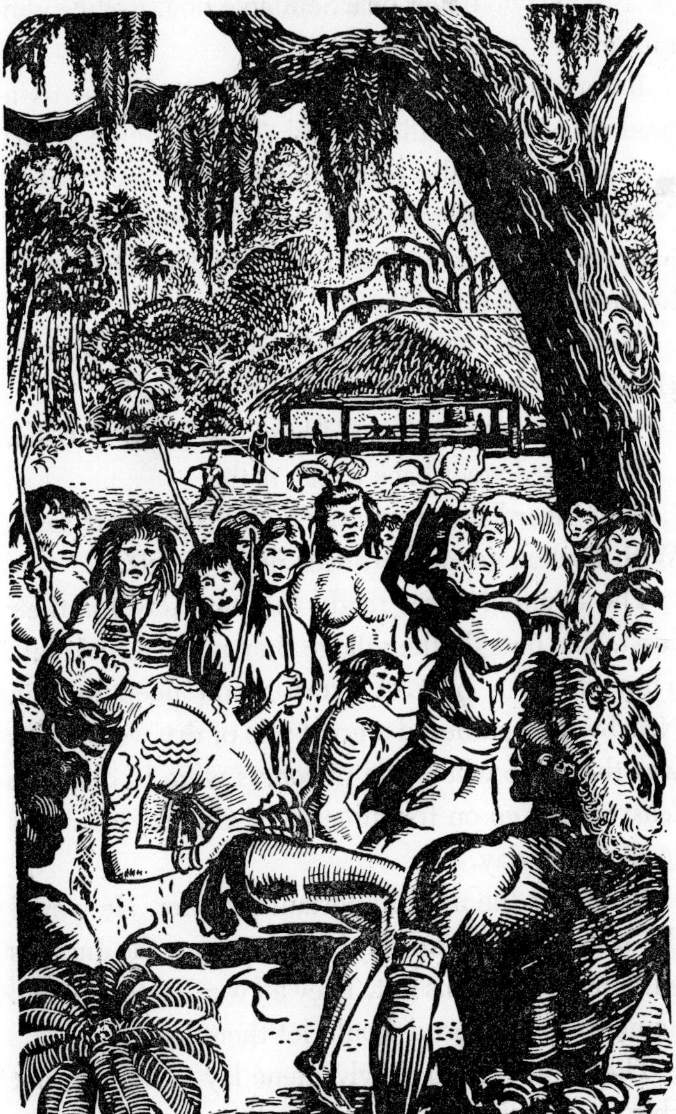

"E-chee will never be a Seminole dog. E-chee will rather die."

Before the warrior could get there, he heard a loud splash. Then all was still. The Seminole guard ran to look. Bubbles came up from the black water. Now other warriors came running to see what had happened. In the bushes they found the Seminole feathers E-chee had worn.

"Fool!" cried a warrior. "He has drowned himself. He would rather die than be a Seminole."

"We should have burned him, too," said Cat-sha.

The guard went back to the path.

René heard the warriors talking. His heart sank. With E-chee gone, there was no hope left.

The Seminoles got ready the next day for their feast. Just outside the village they made a little hill. They drove a post of green wood deep into it. Nearby they gathered a great pile of dry wood. This was the stake where the prisoners were to die. The feast would go on for three days. One prisoner was to die each day.

René was the most important prisoner. He would die last, on the third day. All day long the Indians gathered outside his hut. They all wanted to see him. Sometimes the guard would let them look in.

The hours passed slowly. René lay in his hut, not able to do a thing to save himself.

Chapter 27. E-CHEE BRINGS NEWS

The Alachua village was quiet and happy. The Indians sat before their tents and huts. The hunters had come back with plenty of game. They lay on the grass resting. The squaws were busy getting supper. Children played and ran and shouted. Some boys were swimming in the river.

The biggest hut stood in the center of the village. The eagle feathers hanging from it showed the chief lived there. Before this hut were Micco and the other leaders. Eagle, too, was there. Behind Micco stood a tall, slender lad wearing the flamingo feather. The older men smoked their pipes and talked. The young men spoke only when they were asked a question.

At last Micco turned to the boy behind him.

"What do you think, Has-se?" he asked. "Can the white men be enemies among themselves? Would some white men fight other whites?"

"I think that can be, my father. Our Indian tribes are often enemies. Why not the whites?"

"Well spoken, my son," said Micco. "You are right.

I fear what we have heard is true. If it is, I am sorry. Our white brothers are dead."

The news of Don Pedro's attack had come that day. The Indian runner had told of the Spaniards' coming and of the fight. He told, too, that Ribault's ships had been driven ashore. They had given up to the Spaniards. The Spaniards had killed every last one.

As they talked, the boys in the river began to shout. In a moment they came with a strange young warrior. The boys brought him to Micco. A boy spoke up.

"This warrior came down the river in a canoe. He asked us about the Alachuas. He wants to see Micco the chief."

"I am Micco," said the chief to the young brave. "Who are you? What do you wish?"

"I am E-chee," said the young Indian. "I look for your son, Has-se."

"This is he. What do you want with him?"

Greatly surprised, Has-se stepped forward. The stranger took from his breast a flamingo feather. It was just like the one in Has-se's hair.

Handing it to Has-se, E-chee said, "The one who sends this is in great danger. He asks that you help him."

Has-se took the feather eagerly. "It comes from

Ta-lah-lo-ko, the young white chief! Where is he?"

E-chee now told how the Spaniards had killed his people. He told how they had taken Fort Caroline. Then he told how he had been captured.

"And they caught Ta-lah-lo-ko, too," he said. "I was able to get away. The young white chief is soon to die. The Seminoles will burn him at the stake."

Has-se's eyes flashed. He turned to Micco.

"My father, I must help him," he said. "He is my best friend and my brother. I would die for him."

"If he still lives, he shall be saved," cried Micco. He turned to E-chee.

"Do you know the way? Can you lead us to these Seminole wolves? Are you strong enough to go right back?"

"I know the way," said E-chee. "I am ready to go."

"Good!" cried the old chief. He turned to Eagle, his son-in-law. "Take twenty braves, Eagle," he said. "Go to this Seminole village. If Ta-lah-lo-ko still lives, save him. Come back with him. I fear to send more men. If you had more, you would attack the Seminoles. They know the swamp too well. Our whole tribe and the Alachuas could not beat them there. You must be cunning. But learn the way. If we can wipe them out, we will go back later. Now we need speed."

Eagle was only too glad to go. In an hour he had

picked his twenty and was ready to start. Has-se was the first one ready.

E-chee, who was to show the way, had eaten. He felt like a new man and was ready for anything.

The little band jumped into their canoes. Swiftly they paddled up the river toward the great swamp.

E-chee was in the first canoe with Eagle and Has-se. As they paddled, he told them more of his story. He told them how he had got away.

"I knew that I must leave quickly to save him," he said. "I made up my mind to try that first night. I knew I could not get past their guard on the path. I tried my plan as soon as it was dark.

"I found a piece of heavy, water-soaked wood. I carried it near the path. I threw my Seminole feathers into the bushes. Then I sang a death song. I threw the wood into the water. It sank. Quietly I crept to the path. When the guard left, I slipped down the path. They thought I had killed myself. I knew where they had hidden the canoes. I found them. I jumped into one. Night and day I have paddled to find you."

"If only we are not too late," said Has-se.

They dug their paddles deep into the dark water and made the canoe fly.

Chapter 28. HAS-SE TO THE RESCUE

The Seminoles were having their feast. They had started the same day E-chee got to Micco's camp. For two days René had listened to their screaming and howling. The drums beat day and night. The dancing seemed never to stop. Above all he heard the screams of the white prisoners. René knew well what was happening. Only the guard came to the hut now. He still brought food and water every day.

Once Chitta had looked in today. He had smiled. "I wonder how brave you will be when you die," he said. "Well, tomorrow we shall see."

That was all he said. René knew what he meant. His turn had come. The other two prisoners had been killed. The Seminoles would have their fun with him tomorrow.

Could he stand it? Could he hold out to the end? Or would he, too, scream for mercy as the others had done? He threw himself down. He beat the ground with his fists.

"No," he said to himself. "Come what may, I will die like a man. They would be glad to see me beg. I'll show them how a white man dies. I'll not cry out."

He even smiled when the guard brought his food. The guard looked at him in surprise. "He does not know what is coming," he thought. "He'll look different at the stake."

René ate his meal. The guard came back in and freed his legs. He led him outside. A big warrior walked on each side. Now they made him lead a parade around the village. The drums were beating and the Indians were shouting. Everybody was to have a chance to see him.

The parade passed near the guard on the path. He, too, wanted a look at the last prisoner. He stepped forward to see better.

He was gone from the path only a moment. But in that moment three shadows slipped past him into the bushes. The parade passed on. The guard stepped back to his place. He did not know three pairs of sharp eyes were watching him. E-chee, Has-se, and Eagle had come.

They had not stopped once on the way. E-chee had led them into the swamp to the village. No one had stopped them. All the Seminoles were at the feast. Eagle had stopped his men and had gone closer with Has-se and E-chee.

For some time they had lain in the bushes. Then the parade had come by and given them their chance. Now they waited for the Seminoles to go to sleep. Black clouds came over the sky. The moon and stars were blotted out. The air grew heavy. A flash of lightning struck nearby. Then a storm broke loose. They could move quickly now.

E-chee led them back of the village to René's hut. The lightning flashes showed the warrior on guard. E-chee fitted an arrow to his bow and watched him. If the guard heard anything, E-chee would shoot. Then they would grab René and run for it. First, though, they would try another plan.

While E-chee watched, Eagle and Has-se slipped around the back. They took their knives and began to cut their way into the hut. The rain beat down and kept any one from hearing them. They worked slowly but quietly. At last they cut through the wall.

René had thrown himself down after the parade. He had lain awake a long time, but at last he fell asleep. Suddenly he sat up, wide awake. He had heard some one whisper his name.

"Ta-lah-lo-ko!"

Could he be dreaming? The whisper came again.

"Ta-lah-lo-ko!"

"I am here," he whispered.

He heard a little noise. Then some one was beside him. He felt the knife cutting the ropes from his arms and legs.

"It is Has-se. You are saved, my brother!"

Has-se pulled him toward the opening. They slipped through. Without a word the four headed for the path.

The guard was in his place. A bright flash of lightning suddenly came. The guard's hair almost rose. Before him, dripping wet, stood E-chee, the lad who had drowned! He opened his mouth to scream. Just as he did, something hit him on the head. He gave a soft grunt and fell into the mud.

Chapter 29. THE ESCAPE

The storm had kept Cat-sha awake. He turned and rolled, but could not sleep. Finally he thought he would see if the guards were on the job. He pulled his robe around him and went out into the storm.

First he went to René's hut. The guard was there and was wide awake.

"Is the prisoner all right?" asked Cat-sha.

"I looked in just before the storm began," said the Indian. "He was sleeping then."

The rain had put out all the camp fires. It would be hard to get a light. So Cat-sha went on. He was sure René had no chance to get away.

Next he went to see the guard on the path. He

was not there. Cat-sha called angrily to him. No answer. Suddenly he stumbled over him. The warrior was still knocked out. He had been hit just a few minutes before.

Cat-sha shook him but could not bring him to. Could the lightning have hit him? Was he sick? Could an enemy have hit him? Perhaps some one had got on the island. Cat-sha was sure now something was wrong.

Was his prisoner safe? He had to be sure. He left the guard lying in the mud and ran for René's hut again. He would see with his own eyes. He got a dry piece of wood and found a small fire still burning. One look inside told him the story. The hut was empty. The ropes were lying on the floor. The hole in the wall showed how René had got out.

Cat-sha could hardly believe his eyes. They had been saving the young white chief to finish the feast. He was Cat-sha's own prisoner. Cat-sha knew he could not have got loose alone. Somebody had got into his village. Cat-sha leaped from the hut. The guard still stood outside. Even now he did not know René was gone. Cat-sha was so angry he felled him with one blow.

"Seminoles up!" he shouted. "The prisoner is gone!"

The Indians piled out of their beds. They looked

everywhere in the village. Cat-sha wasted no time. He got his best warriors together quickly. He led them down the trail at a run. Any one who got away would head for the canoes. If they could catch him before he got there, all would be well. If he made it to the canoes, he could get away. Cat-sha ran to the canoes to head him off.

They did not know their enemies had passed only fifteen minutes earlier. They did not know how slowly they had to go. Just after they got started, René's swollen ankles got worse. For days the ropes had been tight around them. As he ran, they began to hurt. When they got to their friends, he sank to the ground. He could move no farther.

"Come," cried Eagle, "they may be after us. Two warriors pick up Ta-lah-lo-ko. Carry him. Has-se, stay close by him. E-chee, come with me. You and I will guard the rear. If they catch up, we will fight them off."

The storm had passed by now. The full moon came out and lit their way. E-chee and Eagle looked back often as they hurried on. The moon helped them, but it would also help the Seminoles.

Finally they reached the end of the path. Here they had left their canoes. Everybody breathed easier. They were almost safe now. Eagle kept hurrying them. Carefully they laid René in the first

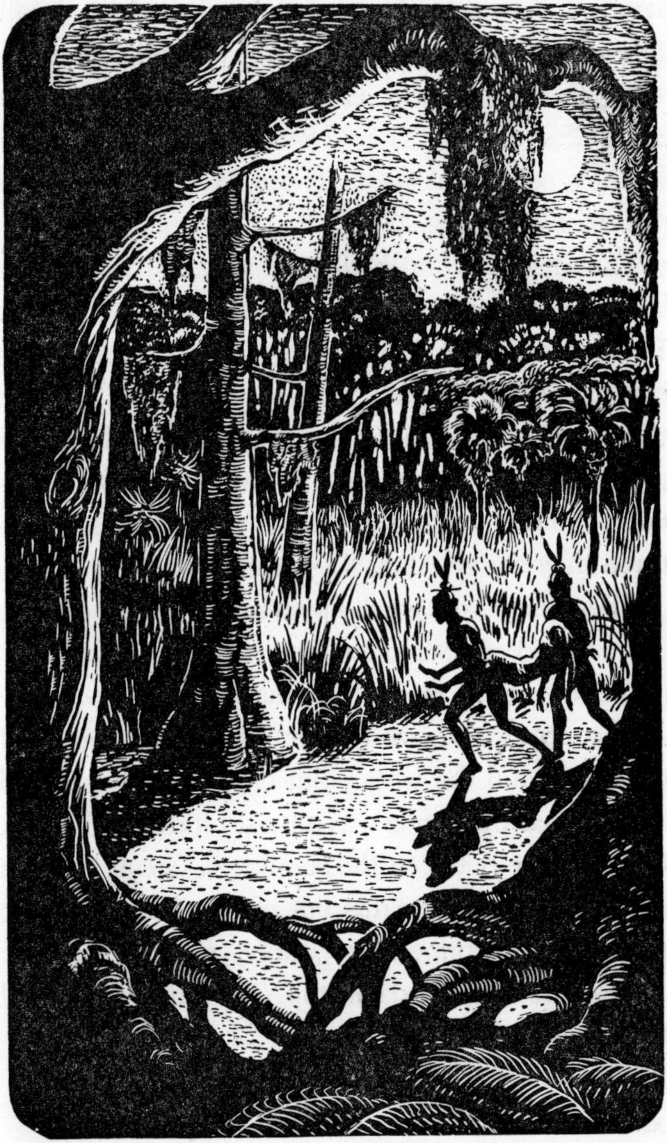

canoe. Two warriors stepped in and paddled off. The others got in their canoe now and followed.

Eagle, Has-se, and E-chee now pulled out the Seminoles' canoes. They drove great holes in them so they could not float. Those in the water they pushed from shore.

They had just finished the last canoe when they heard an angry cry. The Seminoles had spied them. They saw the warriors paddling away. At first they did not see the three who stayed behind. These three now jumped into the only canoe left. Eagle gave it a push. It shot out into the water. The Seminoles shouted and rushed to get their canoes. These three they could catch, they were sure.

Then they saw what happened to their canoes. They yelled and screamed and shook their fists.

"Shoot them!" roared Cat-sha.

The arrows whizzed after the three. Many hit the canoe and the water. But one flew straight and true. Just as the canoe was almost hidden, it landed. It hit Has-se between the shoulders. Going through his body, the point came out of his chest. He gave a sharp cry, dropped his paddle, and fell forward. The others did not dare stop. They raced on until they caught their friends.

Chapter 30. A FAITHFUL FRIEND DIES

Has-se lay dying. René sat beside him, holding his hand. His heart was broken. Has-se was his true friend, his best friend. René loved him more than he could love a brother.

"Oh, Has-se, Has-se!" he cried. "You gave your life for me. It is my fault you are lying here."

"Do not sorrow, Ta-lah-lo-ko, my brother. A brave warrior does not fear death. I did what was right. I don't mind."

"Has-se, we will miss you so much."

"Let me say something about that. I am going to ask you a favor."

"Ask it. If I can do it, I will," said René.

The dying boy smiled. He spoke in a whisper now. He was sinking fast.

"You have lost your people," he said. "My people are losing a son. Take my place. Be a son to my father, Micco. Be a brother to Day Star, my sister. And—please—will you wear the flamingo feather now?"

"Gladly will I be your father's son. Gladly will I be a brother to your sister. I hope they want me.

But did you not say the flamingo feather was only for a chief or his son?"

"But you will be. The flamingo feather means the son will never leave his father—until death. Will you wear it?"

"I will, Has-se! I will!" cried René. "I will stay with him."

The dying boy smiled again. A moment later the end came. They laid his body in a canoe. Sadly they started again for the land of the Alachuas.

Has-se never knew who had shot the arrow. When they took it out of his body, the others found out. The picture of a snake was on the arrow. The arrow was Chitta's—Chitta the snake. So Chitta did get even for his overthrow at the Ripe Corn Feast.

Their return was a sad one. When the Indians saw René, they shouted happily. But then they saw the warriors had on black paint. Black paint meant death. Everybody was quiet.

They carried Has-se to his father. The old man sat hanging his head. The women began to moan.

They laid Has-se to rest as their people always did. They covered his body with great tree trunks. Beside him they laid the things he liked best. Young Indian girls threw wild flowers over him. René put a flamingo feather into his hand. The old chief took René's hand. Then he spoke so all could hear.

"I have lost a son," he said. "But I have a new son. Has-se has gone. Ta-lah-lo-ko has come in his place. Your chief has spoken. This white boy is now the son of your chief."

Day Star took René's other hand. She kissed his forehead.

"I welcome you, Ta-lah-lo-ko, as a brother."

As she spoke, she gave him another flamingo feather. René took it.

"I wear this feather as the chief's son," he said. "I know what it means. I promised Has-se to wear it. I will be Micco's son. I will never fail him. Only death will part us."

And so René became an Indian. The flamingo feather showed he was the chief's son. He soon became a fine hunter. From the Indians he learned to live in the woods. He, too, taught the Indians what the white men knew. Before long René was widely known as a wise leader.

Sometimes the Indians heard stories about the cruel Spaniards. When they could, the Spaniards killed the Indians. Micco's tribe did not go back. They stayed with the Alachuas. The two tribes got along well together. When the Alachua chief died, Micco became chief of both tribes. Eagle and René were his right-hand men.

After Has-se died, Micco sent his warriors to wipe

out the Seminoles. When they got to the swamp, the Seminoles had gone. They had found out the warriors were coming and had left. The Alachuas tore down the Seminole village. They had no more trouble for a long time.

René had now been with the Indians many months. Once he led a hunting party to the great swamp. They sat one night around the fire, smoking and talking. Suddenly they saw a flash of light. A shot rang out. The sound came from some trees nearby. The Indians were scared. René knew it was a gun shot.

A loud cry of pain followed the shot. René ran to the trees. There he found a young Indian rolling in pain. Near him lay the pieces of a Spanish gun. René guessed what had happened. The Indian had tried to shoot one of his men. The gun was old and rusty. It had burst into pieces. The burning powder had put out the Indian's eyes.

His face was badly burned, but René knew him. He told the Indians what had happened.

"He tried to kill us," they said. "Now we will kill him."

"No," said René. "I know him. He is too bad to kill. Let him live. It would be kind to kill him. Take him out in the woods. Leave him there. His people will find him. He will always be blind."

That is what they did. Later Eagle spoke to René. "Who was he?" he asked.

"Chitta the Seminole," said René.

Chapter 31. THE FRENCH COME AGAIN

Three years had passed since the Spaniards had come. Fort Caroline was gone. Saint Augustine was three years old. These were three bad years for the Indians who lived near the Spaniards. They were three happy years for the Alachuas. Micco's people were now a large tribe. They had big fields of corn, pumpkins, and other crops. The forests were full of game. The rivers had plenty of fish. The hunters could always find food.

How could any one be unhappy here? But one was. And he was their chief. They called him Ta-lah-lo-ko. Yes, René was now their chief. The Indians loved him and obeyed him.

René longed to visit his country, France. It seemed he would never again be able to. That made him sad. His Indian friends knew something was wrong. They thought he was troubled by a bad spirit. The old medicine men tried to cure him, but could not. They did not know their chief was homesick.

When Micco died, Eagle was next in line to be chief. The Indians were going to make him their leader. But Eagle would not take it.

"No," he said. "I am not so wise as Ta-lah-lo-ko. He is young, but he is wise. He will be a better leader. Let us make him our chief."

Much to René's surprise the Indians did so. He did not know just what to do. But he was both brave and kind. Before long the Indians all loved him. René worked hard for his people. The tribe was happy and lived well.

But René could not forget his own white people. Then, suddenly, exciting news came. An Indian runner from the coast came to the village.

"The French have come again," he told the Alachuas. "Three great ships flying the lily flag are there. Soon there will be fighting. The French will fight the bad white men of Saint Augustine. My tribe asks that the Alachuas come. The great Alachua chief Ta-lah-lo-ko can drive the Spaniards away. Then his Indian brothers will have peace."

"I will come," said René. "I will bring a hundred warriors." He jumped up. "Bow bearer, call the wise men of our tribe. Bring Eagle. Tell the warriors to get ready. We go to help the French."

The older men came at René's call. The warriors got their bows and arrows ready. When Eagle came, the men sat down to make plans. No word was spoken until all sat down. The pipes were lighted. Then René stood up.

"Wise men of the Alachuas," he said, "listen to me. Many moons ago I, Ta-lah-lo-ko, came to you. You welcomed me. I was glad to be one of you. Now I must go. My own people have come again. I have long wanted to see them. The flamingo feather holds me no longer. Micco is dead. I am sorry to go. If I can, I will come back some day. Now I must go to my own people. First we may have much fighting to do. They ask our help. I will lead our warriors there. When the fighting is done, they will come back. I must go to my country. Until I come back Eagle will be your chief. I, Ta-lah-lo-ko, have spoken."

René sat down. Eagle and others jumped up.

"Do not leave us!" they cried. "We are your people now. You are one of us."

René's heart was touched, but he would not change his mind. When they saw he really wanted to go, they said no more against it. "But come back soon," they begged.

So René led his hundred warriors away. As the canoes shot up the river, the other Indians gathered on the shore. They gave a great cry as René left. He turned and waved good-bye.

Chapter 32. RENÉ JOINS THE FRENCH

René's Indians moved fast. Never before had they made the trip so quickly. When one man tired, another paddled. René remembered many places he and Has-se had passed years before.

Finally they came to the river's end. René's heart jumped. Three tall ships lay about a mile before them. The lily flags were flying in the breeze. French ships! René had not dared hope he would ever see them again. That French flag was his country's flag. He had not seen it since the Spaniards had torn it down at Fort Caroline.

René pointed to a hill. "Wait here," he said. "Make camp. I will go talk to the French chief."

His canoe started across the open water. As they came closer, René saw many eyes watching him. At last a voice from the flag ship called out.

"Halt! What do you want?"

René's men held the canoe still. René stood up. He called out in French:

"Who is captain here? Where can I find him?"

A man, beautifully dressed, stepped to the rail. He was surprised to hear his own language.

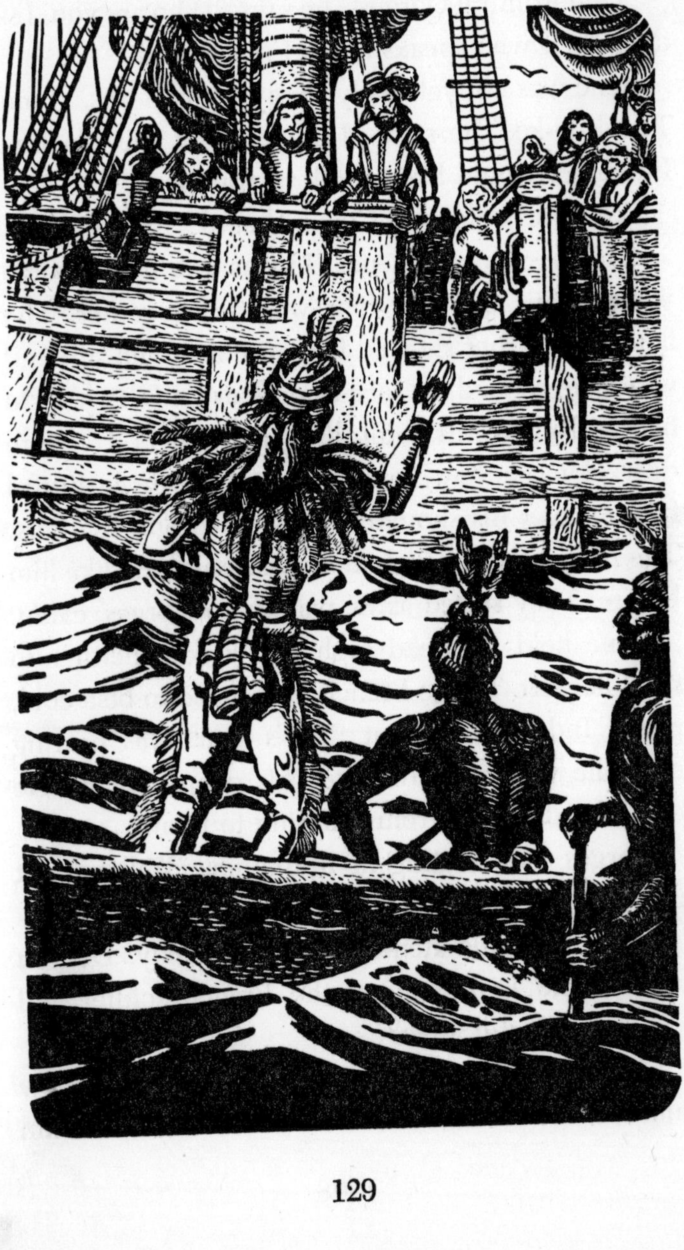

"I am Admiral Gorges," he said. "Who are you, Indian chief who speaks like a Frenchman?"

René was not yet ready to say who he was. "I am Ta-lah-lo-ko," he said. "I am chief of the Alachua Indians. I would like to talk to you alone."

"You are welcome. Come aboard," said Gorges.

All eyes were on René. He was a tall, handsome young man. His long hair was tied together. The flamingo feather showed he was chief. The sun and wind had tanned his face as dark as an Indian's. He had on Indian war paint, like his warriors. He wore deer skin clothes, soft as velvet, with beautiful fringe. Over his shoulders he wore bright feathers. The French sailors had never seen anything like him before. They stared as he walked to Gorges' cabin.

René held his head high. He looked neither to right nor left. To the French he seemed to be a cold, proud Indian chief. But René's heart was beating hard, he was so glad to see his people again. He could hardly keep from shouting to them.

Gorges was waiting in the cabin. "Will you sit down?" he asked.

"Oh, sir," cried René. "Tell me quickly. Do you know René Laudonnière, the French soldier and sailor? Is he still alive?"

"Why, yes," said the surprised Gorges. "I know him well. He is alive. It is because of him that I am here. But there are tears in your eyes. What have you to do with Laudonnière?"

René had sunk into a chair. He put his face into his hands. Now he looked up. "He is my uncle, but he has been a father to me. I am René, his nephew."

When he heard that name, Gorges sprang to his feet. He looked hard at René. "What? Do I hear right? Are you really René? Are you not an Indian? Your uncle thinks you are dead. It has made him a sad old man. Oh, this is good news! I'm glad I came here."

Gorges wanted to tell everybody who René was. "Tell no one yet. I have other things to say to you first," said René.

"Go on," said Gorges.

"I am René—yes. But I am also Ta-lah-lo-ko, the Alachua chief. I have brought a hundred warriors. They are to help you. Why are you here, and how can I help? Tell me your plans."

"I'll do that gladly," said Gorges. "Let me tell you my story. The Spaniards caught me and threw me into prison. Then they made me a slave on their ships. I was able to escape and get back to France. There I met my old friend Laudonnière again. He told me what Don Pedro and the Spaniards had done over here. I wanted to do anything to pay back these Spaniards. I thought there might still be some

French alive here. Well, I sold all I owned. I used the money to buy three ships. So here I am. I got here ten days ago. When the Spaniards saw us they thought we were Spanish, too. But Saint Augustine is too strong for us. I sailed north to the River of May. They had built forts on both sides of the river. You remember the sand bar? Well, I could not get my ships across. I sent my men in small boats. First we took one fort, then the other. The Indians helped a lot. When we landed, they joined us. They want to get rid of the Spaniards. The Spaniards called their forts there Fort Saint Matthew. I have blasted them to the ground. That pays them back for Fort Caroline. I sailed north, then, to this place. We are getting ready to sail back to France."

René now told his story of Fort Caroline, the Seminoles, and the Alachuas. Gorges listened eagerly.

"You have had wonderful adventures! I wish I could have been with you!" he cried.

Gorges now took René on deck. He had his men meet him. The men could hardly believe this Indian chief was one of their own people.

Chapter 33. TREASURE!

"And what," asked Gorges, "do you want to do?"

"I'm going along back to France," said René. "I want to see my uncle. Will you take me?"

"That I will," said Gorges. "But are you willing to give up what you have? You are a great chief here."

"I would rather be a poor man and live with my own people. You, too, love your country. I long thought I would never see France again."

"I know how you feel, lad. Remember I was a Spanish prisoner. Well, let's go. We can sail now if you are ready."

"Will you wait two days longer?" asked René. "My uncle had some papers which I hid. I would like to find them. I am sure he needs them."

"Take as long as you want," said Gorges. "If you wish, I'll go with you. I would like to see the place again. The Spaniards said no one could take their forts. The ships can meet us at the mouth of the river."

"Good," said René.

"I think you are right about the papers," said

Gorges. "I know he is making some claims in court. He told the court his papers were lost at Fort Caroline. He has lost much of what he had. Maybe these papers are the ones he needs."

René was worried to hear his uncle was in need. "Maybe I can help him," he thought. "I will be sure to get these papers."

The next morning René and Gorges rowed out to the Alachuas' camp. Gorges saw how much the Indians loved their white chief.

"I don't know," he said. "Maybe you had real happiness here."

"Yes," said René, "I did. But, after all, I am a white man."

That night they camped at the hill where the Seminoles had once captured René. The next morning René, Eagle, E-chee, and Gorges went up to the fort. They found it torn down and burned to the ground. René was sorry to see it that way.

"I guess it's better than letting the Spanish have it," he said.

They began to search the river bank for the opening to the tunnel. But the bark cover was gone. At last René found the opening. Somebody had blocked it with a great stone. It took all four to pull it loose.

René knew then that some one had found the tunnel. That could mean only the Spaniards.

"They have been here," he said. "I guess there's no hope of finding the papers. Let's make sure, though."

They lit some pine branches and René led the way in.

"I wish I had known this was here," said Gorges. "I could have blown the fort up under them."

They soon reached the place where René had piled the papers. They were gone.

"I buried an iron box," said René. "Maybe they did not find it." He poked his dagger along the tunnel wall. After a few minutes the point hit metal. Here they dug. The box, dirty and rusty, was still there.

"These were his most important papers," said René. "Shall we go?"

"Let's see the rest of the tunnel," said Gorges.

"All right," said René. He started out again. Suddenly they found themselves in a large room.

"This was not here before," said René. "The Spaniards must have dug it out. Look! What's this?"

René was pointing to some wood and iron chests. They were piled from floor to roof. On each one was the coat of arms of the Spanish king. René and Gorges tried to lift one. It was far too heavy.

"Say!" cried Gorges. "You are in luck, René. Do you know what this is? This is the treasure room of

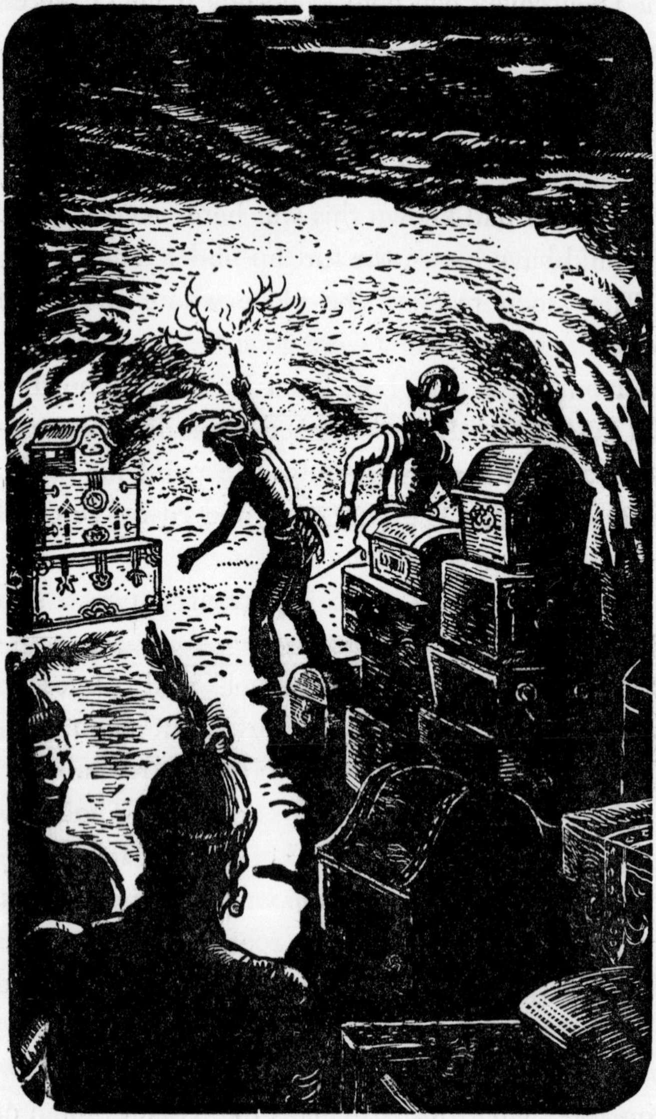

the Spaniards! Right now you are the richest Frenchman in the world."

"No," said René. "It's not mine. It's yours. You took the fort. If it were not for you, the Spaniards would still be here."

"Oh, no," said Gorges. "I did not come for gold. I came to kill some Spaniards. I did not know the tunnel was here. It was your secret. This is your gold."

"Well," said René, "let's not count our chickens too soon. We can talk about it later. Let's get the chests on the ships."

"Right," said Gorges. "The Spaniards at Saint Augustine may come after us any time."

The tide was so high that day, the ships were able to get over the bar. They lay at the mouth of the river. The men carried the chests on board. There were so many they had to work all day to get them all. By evening they were done and ready to sail.

René now said good-bye to his Indians. One by one the warriors came and kissed his hand. René had a kind word for every man.

As long as they were there he wore his Indian clothes. The flamingo feather still showed in his hair.

The ships now moved slowly away. The Indians waved from their canoes. The white sails filled. Long after they had crossed the bar René stood at the rail.

He watched the shore grow dim. As night came, he turned and went into the cabin. When he came out, he looked like a stranger. He wore white men's clothes once more. The flamingo feather was gone.

That night they opened the Spanish chests. The chests were filled with jewels, gold coin, and silver. They could not even guess how much it was worth.

"They found the tunnel," said René. "The books and papers they must have burned. Then they thought the tunnel would be a good hiding place. When you took the fort they had no time to save their gold."

They talked again about who should have the treasure. At last Gorges agreed to take enough to pay for his ships and men. "The rest," he said, "belongs to you, René. That's the way it's going to be."

And that is the way it was. So a poor boy suddenly became a very rich young man.

* * *

René bought back his old home. He and his uncle lived there long and happily. Often he thought of his Indian friends. We do not know much more about René. It is sure that he did once more go back to America. Whether he stayed, no one knows. We do know that for many years his family carefully kept the suit of an Indian chief. To it was fastened, with a gold chain and pin, a red feather.